W9-BVU-319

DISCARD

Underwater

by DEBBIE LEVY

For my husband, Rick Hoffman,
for being there underwater, over water,
and the many places in between.

Text copyright © 2007 by Debbie Levy

Design by Kelly Rabideau and Shae I. Strunk

Cataloging-in-Publication

Levy, Debbie.
Underwater / by Debbie Levy.
    p. ; cm.
ISBN 978-1-58196-053-2
Summary: Sixth-grader Gabe, a middle child, is unsure of himself and
how he fits in his family and the rest of his world. His oldest brother has
learning disabilities, does he? Is he a "difficult child," as the book his mom
has suggests? Or does he simply need to find his place?
1. Self-confidence—Juvenile fiction. 2. Identity (Psychology)—Juvenile fiction.
3. Middle-born children—Juvenile fiction. [1. Self-confidence—Fiction.
2. Identity—Fiction. 3. Middle-born children—Fiction.] I. Title.
PZ7.L58257 Un 2007
[Fic] dc22
OCLC: 84840996

Published by DARBY CREEK Publishing
7858 Industrial Parkway
Plain City, OH 43064
www.darbycreekpublishing.com

Cover and jacket printed in Italy
Interior printed in U.S.A.

1 2 3 4 5 6 7 8 9

Contents

Chapter One

Victor and Me

I'm deep underwater, so deep there's no sunshine, no waves, no gulls—just me, my oxygen tank, and my flashlight. And my diving buddy, Victor. We can't see much farther than five feet from our masks. Poisonous stingrays suddenly appear in our line of sight, and we know there are sharks in these waters. But we swim on, because we also know—based on the careful research I did before we made this dive—that the remains of the *U.S.S. Victoriana* are somewhere around here.

At least, we're pretty sure we know this.

Yes, we strongly believe the wreck is in the area.

Well, we think so.

Let me put it this way: We hope so. We hope so because we'd like to be the first people to reach the *Victoriana*, which is supposed to be filled with millions of dollars' worth of jewelry, gold coins, and silver. But we also hope so because we only have ten minutes of air left, and if there's one thing we've learned from earlier dives, it's the importance of getting back to the surface slowly.

I keep saying we and, of course, I mean me and my buddy Victor. Victor lives, so to speak, in my computer. This is a good thing and a bad thing. The good thing about it is that when I want him to go away, all I have to do is turn off the *DeepSea Danger Hunt* game, and, *click*, he disappears. I wouldn't mind if it was that easy to make some other people I know disappear.

Victor has this annoying habit, which I know he can't help. He's just programmed to say dumb things, like giving obvious advice when we're in tight spots.

"Remember, Gabe, we're out of poison darts, so if there's a shark around, stay very still."

Ya think?

Victor's so busy offering useless advice that he sometimes forgets to tell me stuff that would really help me out. Like on our last dive, he didn't say anything when our tanks were empty. Instead, he just made the thumbs-up sign. (That means "going up!") So I sped to the surface way too fast, which caused nitrogen bubbles to form in my bloodstream, which resulted in my painful death. My virtual death, that is. Which is why, now, with five minutes of oxygen left, I start getting my stuff together so I can get to the surface safely.

The bad thing about Victor being just a guy inside my

computer—a creation of little pixels and computer code—is that I can't make him listen to me when I have something to say. Sometimes I wish I could, though. It would be cool if he could listen, because sometimes I feel like I've got so much to say that I'm going to explode.

Am I the only kid who feels like that? And the only one who feels like time is moving way too slowly, and I'm never going to grow up and be independent and successful and, hopefully, hugely famous? I feel like that a lot. It's not even really that I'm in such a huge hurry to be an adult. It's just that sometimes I'm so ready not to be a kid. Because being a kid can be such a pain.

Like most days after school, the other kids in the neighborhood play pick-up games of soccer in the street. Me, I don't like soccer. I'm not good at soccer, and I don't care about getting good at soccer. My mom's always dropping hints about how I should go outside and get some fresh air—code for Gabe, you should go play soccer.

I care about deep-sea diving. I love the idea of exploring underwater and seeing all kinds of weird sea creatures and discovering shipwrecks. I'm thinking of becoming an oceanographer, maybe even being the next Jacques Cousteau. "Gabe Livingston," people will say. "He's a young Jacques Cousteau."

If I'm going to be the next Jacques Cousteau, why

should I waste my time running after a soccer ball?

I have to admit I don't have much experience in deep-sea exploration, or even shallow-water exploration. Actually, I don't have any experience. None at all. I've never been scuba diving, or even snorkeling. The closest I've gotten is hanging out at Tanks for You, a store in the shopping center near our house, where they sell aquariums and tropical fish. And—I think this counts for something—I like to swim at our neighborhood pool. Swimming is the only sport I do, and it's the only team I don't hate being on. I'm pretty good at breaststroke, and I'm very good at holding my breath underwater.

Then there's this *DeepSea Danger Hunt* game, my other connection to the underwater world. It's a complicated game. You have to make smart decisions based on knowledge of the undersea landscape and creatures that live there, and then use that intelligence to stay alive in the game. I can play for hours and not get bored.

Then again, sometimes I feel like I'm going to explode because time is moving too quickly, not too slowly, and I'm growing up too fast, and before I know it I'll be old enough to drive, to vote, and to go to college—and it'll turn out I have no talents at all. None. Whatsoever. I should have played soccer as a kid, and I should have gone along with whatever the other kids did, because they were smart and I was stupid. Not only stupid, but *ridiculous*, with my dreams of being the next Jacques Cousteau by spending all my time on a dumb computer game. I mean, I won't be the next *anybody*.

Well, I've got two minutes and forty-five seconds of oxygen left. I swim to Victor and make the thumbs-up sign (CTRL-U on the keyboard). He nods and we kick our way—slowly, slowly—to the surface. We didn't find the *Victoriana*. But we also didn't get eaten by sharks, stung by rays, or chased off by rival wreck-divers. We'll climb aboard our small craft where John, Alison, and the other citizens of this digital world await us, and we'll head back to the dock. In the lab, we'll plot our expedition on the large map that keeps track of our findings. Then I'll save the game to my computer's hard drive, exit the program, switch off the power, and run out the door, because if I don't start walking, like *now*, I'll be late for school.

Chapter Two

A Group Situation

The last part of morning announcements is the part I dread the most. Today is a good example.

"Finally, this morning, I'd like to congratulate Julie Ferris and Amy Wheeler," our principal, Mrs. Mead says. "Yesterday in the lunchroom Julie cleaned up trash. Thank you, Julie."

Julie's in my class. She tilts her head down a little, as if she's suddenly become shy. That would be, um, unusual. Usually Julie is raising her hand and going, "Ooh-ooh-ooh," because she knows all the answers and always wants the teacher to call on her. Or she's showing off the new moves she's learned in her gymnastics class, which, as she's let everyone know, is only for the best, most talented kids.

So now she's shy.

"As for Amy," Mrs. Mead continues, "she helped one of her classmates who wasn't feeling well get to the nurse's office during recess. Thank you, Amy."

Amy's in my class, too. Julie and Amy are best friends, and you never saw two such perfect people. I think they have special radars built into their heads that are always tuned in to opportunities to be goody-goodies. You think they're just eating lunch or playing basketball or whatever, but really their radars are scanning the area for their next chance to show off. They take turns at it.

Probably, Julie and Amy were both with Cindy Greer on the playground yesterday when Cindy said she had a terrible stomachache and was feeling dizzy and almost passed out. Probably they checked their little goody-goody calendars and saw that it was Amy's turn to show off, since Julie had just cleaned up the lunchroom garbage.

"Hugs to both of these sixth graders," Mrs. Mead continues. She's talking about those little chocolate swirl candies that come wrapped in foil. If your name is announced over the loudspeaker because a teacher has seen you do a good deed, you get a little bag of Hugs. They're part of this program called HUGS that Mrs. Mead started at our school this year. HUGS is supposed to stand for *Helping Unity Grow in School*. I think it stands for *Helping Ugly Girls Suck Up*. If Julie and Amy keep getting Hugs at the rate they've been going, they'll be able to open a candy store by the end of the year.

"America the Beautiful" now blares over the loudspeaker. *"Oh, beautiful, for special girls, of Ferris-Wheeler fame. For purple mountains' majesty, above this stupid place! Oh, Ferris Wheel, oh Ferris Wheel! God shed good grades on thee. . . ."*

Well, that's what plays in my head, anyway.

As the song drones on, I draw pictures on the tiny squares of paper I always keep handy for my flipbooks. I sketch fifteen little Ferris Wheels. In the first picture, two girls are sitting in one of the carts. But as the wheel turns (as I flip the book), the girls lean out of their seats, then lean a bit more, then still more, until they tip right out of the Ferris Wheel and fall tumbling to Earth.

I don't really have anything against the Ferris Wheel. It's just that they know how to be in the right place at the right time. It's nice that Amy helped Cindy to the nurse's office yesterday. Really. It's so nice. But how is it she managed to do her good deed so that three teachers saw it, but when I helped Chris after he threw up on my new sneakers last month, no one saw a thing? Amy gets Hugs and her name mentioned during morning announcements. I get barf-to-go.

Last year when I turned in a stack of new comic books that someone had left on the playground, a teacher complimented me for doing a good deed, but that was before Mrs.

Mead came up with HUGS. No one heard *my* name over the loudspeaker. No one gave *me* candy. And I love comic books, almost as much as computer games. (I'd like to be the next Stan Lee—who created the Fantastic Four, the X-Men, the Incredible Hulk, and Spider Man—but never mind.) It was a really hard decision for me to take the comic books to the office. I thought about keeping them for a couple of days, just long enough to read them, but I didn't. I turned them in—and some of them were double issues.

Announcements are finally over. It's time for science. We're studying ecosystems, and the class is divided into groups of three or four kids. Each group has built its own little world of dirt, water, plants, guppies, tadpoles, bugs, and whatever else grows in tanks made out of big, empty soda bottles. We've built separate sections for water and dirt, with the dirt section sort of nesting above the water section. We observe the eco-columns (that's what they're called) every day and take turns writing our observations down in notebooks. Each group keeps one notebook, so everybody in the group has to agree about what has been observed. Today is Derek's day to write.

"Okay," he says, "we've still got two guppies and that one slug. One of the guppies looks like it's about to have babies. The grasshopper's alive, and so's the earthworm. The beetle died."

Okay, look. I am the first to admit that I'm not the greatest guy in these group things. But none of us has had time yet to eyeball our eco-column, so how Derek can sit there and announce how many guppies, slugs, and whatever we have is a total mystery to me. Not really—obviously, he's making it up.

"Okay, write it down," Zach says. Derek begins writing. He bends his shaggy head over the notebook and plops the hand he's not writing with right on the page so no one can see what he's doing. Not that, say, Zach, cares. He'll go along with anything Derek does.

"Are you sure your observations are correct?" Elise asks.

Go, Elise! She leans in closer and forgets to hold her breath. "Phew!" She gags and jumps back. Ms. Stewart warned us that when you try to keep a slice of nature all wrapped up in a soda bottle for a few weeks, it can raise some serious stink.

So now Elise is no longer interested in whether Derek is right or wrong. But me, I can't stand it.

"Wait a minute, Derek," I say. "We haven't even made our observations yet. We're all supposed to observe as a group before we write anything down. I haven't had a chance to check anything out yet. And I didn't see you observe anything either."

Derek looks up from the notebook without lifting his

pencil (or hand) from the paper. "Well, Gabe," he says, "what you don't know is that my powers of observation are highly developed. It doesn't take me as long as normal sixth-graders to observe an ecosystem. And that means that I can observe much quicker than sixth-grade retards like you."

Our desks are set up face to face, like a line of scrimmage in a football game. Derek has called me a retard before. That time we were out on the playground, and I hit him, hard, right in the shoulder. Then he tripped me and jumped on my legs for a while. I'm not the greatest fighter. I can't start a fistfight here in the classroom—Ms. Stewart would have a fit.

But I'm mad, and I can't stop myself from shoving my desk into Derek's. The pencil pops out of his hand, the notebook falls to the floor, and the edge of the desk knifes into his gut. "Oof!" he says.

I'm sure Derek is now going to do something like shove the desks back in my direction, so I get out of my seat to protect my ribcage. When he sees he can't get me, the rat calls out, "Ms. Stewart, Gabe—"

Just then Ms. Ellis, the teacher assistant assigned to our class, swishes by. She's missed this entire argument between Derek and me. She misses a lot of stuff that goes on between us kids, stuff that never gets past Ms. Stewart. Ms. Ellis seems to be the type of person who gets focused on one thing at a time, which takes up every bit of her attention. Right now she's focused on hurrying over to Ecosystem Group Number 3 (we're Number 5), whose members are jumping up and down about something or another. Maybe they have a tadpole that sprouted legs.

Whatever the reason, Ms. Ellis is practically sprinting across the room. Just as she dashes by me, a fat wad of dollar bills falls out of her pocket. It's the money everyone's brought in for next week's field trip to the art museum. What a wad of cash! It hits the floor and actually takes a bounce because Ms. Ellis has it all rolled up tight with a rubber band. As she runs by, her foot kicks the money ball toward the radiator, where it rolls underneath, barely sticking out. One more kick by someone passing by and that money will roll way, way under the heating unit, far out of reach. If it doesn't get totally ruined from the water that sometimes drips down under there, maybe it will get burned up when the heat kicks in.

As I dive to the floor to save our field trip money, images of Hugs flash in my head. But only for a fraction of a second, because the next thing flashing in my head is a white burst of pain. That, and Derek's voice, yelling, "Owww!"

He saw the wad of dough, too, and dove to the floor to make the big save. We both fight through our pain to struggle for the money, but our collision and resulting scuffle send the money ball careening under the radiator like a hockey puck.

"Idiot!" I yell, springing to my feet.

"Retard!" he shouts, right in my face. That's two retards in five minutes. I lunge at him, and he dodges, but our ecosystem is not so lucky. I knock it off our desks and observe it as it splats on the floor—a miniature world filled with two cups of dirt, half a quart of water, nine rocks, three twigs, a clump of grass, and one slug, one grasshopper, one earthworm, two guppies (the female one with that dark spot that signals she's going to have babies). Oh, and one dead beetle.

Just as Derek had observed.

Chapter Three

I Hate to Tell You

Ms. Stewart seems to believe me when I say I was trying to do a good deed by diving after the money.

"Don't try so hard," she says. She also says, "Both of you to the office!"

We have to wait a few minutes to see Mrs. Mead, who's in a meeting. When she's done, she calls Derek and me into her office.

"What happened?" she says.

"He went crazy is what happened," Derek says.

"He called me a retard," I say.

"Aw, it's just an expression," Derek says.

"Not to me," I say. "Not to the person being called it."

"He was going crazy over our ecosystem," Derek says. "Everyone in our group agreed on our observations, and I was all set to write them down when he shoved the desk into my stomach."

I don't answer this right away, so Mrs. Mead steps in.

"Is that true, Gabe?" she says. "Did you shove the desk into his stomach?"

"Yes, but. . . ." I explain as best I can, but somehow I only end up looking more and more guilty. No wonder people have the right to remain silent when they get arrested.

Derek, on the other hand, could be a lawyer, he's so good at explaining and clearing things up, making himself look good. After Mrs. Mead tells him that it doesn't help her understand the situation if he keeps saying I went "crazy," he moves in a different direction. Suddenly he begins to analyze me, he goes inside my head—he becomes my shrink.

"I think maybe Gabe was frustrated at how quickly I made my scientific observations," he says. "So instead of believing I can work that fast—some of us can—he became angry. I also think Gabe was frustrated because he hasn't gotten a Hug all year. So, both types of frustration came out in inappropriate ways. It would be better for everyone if he could just chill out."

At this point, I'd like to chill out Derek's face. What does he know about me and what I might be frustrated about? Who came and made him Chief Child Psychologist of the sixth grade?

Maybe Mrs. Mead agrees with me. "Derek, why don't you tell me about your part in this instead of guessing about what Gabe might be feeling?"

The young lawyer shifts again, smooth as a finely geared racing bike. "I had looked at our ecosystem before class. So I had already analyzed the stuff in our tank. No one but Gabe argued with me about it. I was just trying to save us time so we'd have longer to work on the graphs we're supposed to make to go along with our observations."

And so Derek rests his case. I, basically, have nothing to add. I mean I do, but I could never get it out so well, so I just stop trying. Mrs. Mead talks to us about teamwork and cooperation, and she reminds Derek that words can hurt as much as fists, and then we're done. As Derek and I are walking out the door, she calls after me. "Gabe, would you stay for another minute, please?"

Derek gives me a smirk and keeps walking. Sighing, I turn and go back into Mrs. Mead's office and take a seat. She closes her door. I hate when that happens.

"Is there anything else you want to talk about?" she says. She's looking at me carefully.

I look back. What does she want me to say? "Uh—not really," I say.

"Nothing? You're ready to walk back into class and start cooperating with Derek and the others?"

I lean forward in my chair. "I hate being called a retard," I say. "And I hate being called crazy."

"I understand," Mrs. Mead says. "Those are thoughtless things to say. And words can hurt."

"I hate it," I say again.

"I hear you," she says. "Why do you hate it so much?"

I feel the tears building up around my eyeballs, but fight them back. "I just do."

"There's always a reason, Gabe."

"Because maybe it sort of runs in my family."

Mrs. Mead looks at me carefully. If I wanted to get touchy about it, I could say that she looks at me like I'm crazy. But I know that's not really what's going on. She's just looking at me.

Then Mrs. Mead taps some keys on her desktop computer. "Let's look at your last report card." She waits a few moments for the information to come up on the screen.

"All As and Bs," she says. "You earned those grades, Gabe. You're a very good student. You must know you're as far from mentally retarded as can be."

I know she's right, but still—what is it with me? Okay, I shouldn't say I'm retarded. I know I'm not, and some kids really are, and I would never make fun of them, unlike certain people I know, named Derek. Okay, so I'm not retarded. But sometimes I feel like I'm—something. Something a little weird. I mean, I dream about doing great and exciting things, about following in the footsteps of great people, but I'm so far from knowing enough, from knowing anything really, that I must be crazy even to have those daydreams.

There's no way I can explain this to Mrs. Mead, so I say, "I hate being called crazy. I know what kids are thinking when they say that—that I'm crazy like Jake. That Jake is a crazy retard and so am I."

Mrs. Mead is shaking her head, but before she can disagree with me, I keep going. "And the same with Maxie. When he's a little older and the crazy things he does don't seem so cute anymore, then we'll all be called crazy retards."

Jake is my older brother. Maxie is my younger brother. Jake graduated from Franklin Elementary School last year, and now he's in seventh grade at the middle school. Maxie and I both go to Franklin—me in sixth grade; Maxie in first.

For as long as I can remember, Jake has had problems in school. When he was in second grade and I was in first grade, I would see him sitting in one of the "trouble chairs" outside Mrs. Mead's door nearly every day when my class walked by the office on the way to the cafeteria. He just couldn't focus on his work, so he was always bothering other kids—making noises, touching them, getting up and walking around the classroom. Halfway through that school year, Jake went to see a special doctor. That doctor, a psychiatrist, met with Jake and my parents a bunch of times. Later, the doctor gave Jake a prescription for medicine that works on his brain to help him focus and be less antsy. He still takes that medicine and has regular appointments with the psychiatrist.

The doctor gave my parents some names for Jake's problems. The big name is Attention Deficit Hyperactivity Disorder—ADHD for short. But what makes school even harder for Jake is that he also had LDs, learning disorders. Basically, that means he doesn't learn the same way other kids do. When he hears a teacher explaining something in school, he doesn't get it right away. It's like the information goes in his ears, and he hears the sounds just fine, but the information takes detours before it sinks in his brain. Same thing with reading—and that LD has its own name, *dyslexia.* For his LDs Jake gets extra help in school.

It turns out that Jake's pretty smart about most things, but it's hard for him to prove it because of the ADHD and his LDs. He's also better in school than he used to be, and he probably won't have to take medicine in a couple more years. The only thing is, now instead of being fidgety, sometimes Jake will space out on you for no apparent reason. "Earth to Jake," kids say when they notice that he's drifted into his own world. I think it's because he's thinking so much about how to turn the world into pictures or sculptures or other types of art. Jake's not only pretty smart, he's also a pretty amazing artist—although I have to say, some of his pictures look to me like the wild insides of a crazy person's head.

As for Maxie, I'm afraid he's on his way to craziness, although no one else seems to notice. For example, two weeks ago he came home with a note from his teacher complaining of his "inappropriate laughter in the rug area."

"What is this, Maxie?" Dad asked when Maxie showed him the note after dinner.

"She's trying to control my life!" Maxie said. Then he went on to explain that his teacher makes them stay totally quiet whenever the class is in the rug area, where they gather for the Pledge of Allegiance, review the day's schedule, and get homework assignments.

Dad said that the teacher needs to be in control of the classroom if twenty-five children are to get anything done. He talked about his own office, where he and the rest of the salespeople have to be quiet when the boss calls a meeting, even though they're all grown-ups.

The problem is Maxie and quiet don't get along. See, everything makes Maxie laugh. Not just cartoons and jokes, but goofy things like flashing lights and music and probably even the Pledge of Allegiance. So that morning Dad told Maxie that no matter what, he must try very hard not to laugh in the rug area.

"Even if someone makes a funny face?" Maxie asked.

"Even if it's a *really* funny face," Dad said.

"Even if it's a *really, really* funny face?" Maxie asked.

"Even if it's *really, really* funny."

"Even like this?" And Maxie made a really, really funny face.

Dad laughed. I didn't.

And I'm not laughing here in the principal's office. Neither is Mrs. Mead. She's frowning. "Oh, Gabe," she says, "you and Jake and Maxie aren't crazy retards." Just saying that—"crazy retards"—makes her flinch. "You and your brothers have the normal share of ups and downs, nothing more and nothing less. I hate to tell you, but you're not so different from most other families. Can you try really hard to believe that?"

I shrug, mutter "okay," and head back to the classroom. As I'm walking, my brain takes over and starts wondering. What *would* it be like if I believed we were normal—just like everybody else?

Well, I think, that would be a good thing and a bad thing. It would be good to be normal and to get along and to have lots of friends and no more explosions. But it would also be bad because I don't think the next Jacques Cousteau is going to be just another person, nothing more and nothing less. I hate to tell you, Mrs. Mead.

Chapter Four

It's a Beautiful Day

Nobody sends a note home about the ecosystem erup-tion, but Maxie's in the same school as me, and somehow he heard about what happened. He gives Mom a detailed report as soon as we walk into the house. She looks a little worried, so I say, "Mom, do I have a note from school?"

She shrugs. "Do you?"

"No. It wasn't important enough to send a note home, which means it isn't important enough to talk about. Maxie just talks too much."

"But, Mom, he had to go to the office—" Maxie starts.

"That's enough, Maxie. It's Gabe's story, and you're starting to sound like a tattletale. And, Gabe, you know something can be worth talking about even if your teacher doesn't send home a note about it."

It's my turn to shrug now. "Okay," I say.

Then Mom turns to Jake, who gets home from middle

school about the same time Maxie and I get home from Franklin. "Hey, big guy," she says. "How was your day?"

"Fine," he says. "I need a snack."

"Okay," Mom says. "Anyone else? Gabe, Maxie?"

"Peanut butter crackers," Maxie says.

"I'm not hungry," I say.

Maxie's peanut-butter-cracker-eating routine is enough to take away anyone's appetite. He splits the crackers apart and peels the thin layer of peanut butter off. He piles the twelve scraped-off crackers on one side of his plate and the twelve peanut butter pancakes on the other. Then he smushes the peanut butter layers together and eats them all in one bite—one big glob that he has to roll around his mouth forever before he can swallow it. His next trick is to divide the orange-colored crackers into groups—one day it'll be two at a time, another day three at a time, up to six crackers—and eat them smushed together in one mouthful. I hate peanut butter crackers.

I head upstairs to my room. What I really want to do is get on the computer, but the computer isn't in my room. It's in a little room right off the kitchen, and I don't feel like being near Maxie and Jake right now. I don't want to have to explain my game to Jake, and I don't want to have to deal with Maxie begging for a turn and accidentally spewing orange crumbs every time he says, "Please?"

Sitting at my desk, I gather a stack of paper that I've already cut for flipbooks. I draw a bunch of pictures showing a small boy with a big, round head. The boy in the pictures is eating crackers, but not peanut butter crackers. Just plain, round crackers. As he eats, his small body gets bigger and his big head gets smaller, until he is all body and zero head. In the last frame, the boy explodes. I know what you're thinking, but it's not Maxie. What do I care that he tattled to Mom about my trip to the principal's office?

A flipbook takes a long time to make and a few seconds to use. I flip through the exploding boy book one more time and then move to my bed, where I reach for a small paperback book on my nightstand. *Handbook for the New Aquarist*, it's called. On the cover is a photograph of brightly colored fish swimming around in a sparkling clean aquarium tank. The back cover says:

> Congratulations! As a new aquarist, you are about to immerse yourself in a world that is usually invisible to humans—the peaceful, shimmering world of underwater. You'll find fish of every color, fish with different "personalities," fish that race around, fish that float languidly.
>
> With the right equipment and care, an aquarium can provide many years of enjoyment to its owner and long life to the fish that call it home. This book will help you become one of the millions of people who enjoy the magical underwater world.
>
> So jump on in—the water's fine!

Ha, ha, right? That last sentence just makes you want to read the book cover to cover, doesn't it?

I really like tropical fish, so my parents have said that I can get a tank and set up my own aquarium. First, though, I'm supposed to read up on aquariums so I know what to do. The problem is most books about aquariums are incredibly boring. When I see chapter headings like *Choosing a Filtration System* or *Dealing with Algae*, I almost want to forget the whole idea. And if authors think it helps to throw in clever little expressions like "jump on in—the water's fine!"—well, it doesn't.

The only good part of the book is the section in the middle with pages and pages of color pictures of tropical fish. With all their stripes and patterns and colors and shapes, they look like living pieces of art. Plus, they have great names: angelfish, tiger barb, skunk catfish, silver dollar, swordtail, clown loach. Then there are the Siamese fighting fish and the kissing gourami. I wonder how those two would get along in a tank together.

Instead of reading about aquariums, I'd rather talk about fish with someone like Dominique, the guy who works at the aquarium store. He knows tons about tropical fish—freshwater fish, saltwater fish, coral reefs, everything. He comes from a different country—Guadeloupe, which is part of France, even though it's in the Caribbean Sea—where people go snorkeling all the time. Dominique told me that when he was a kid he would just head to the beach with his swim mask and snorkel tube and dive into a strange, quiet world of color and movement. He said that on the surface the water looked like a giant greenish-blue plate. But once you broke the surface, you were in a whole different world.

I can tell by the way his voice gets when he talks about it how much Dominique likes to dive into that other world. But here he is, living miles from any ocean at all and almost two thousand miles from the nice, warm, tropical sea he's used to.

"My parents' jobs brought them here," he told me. "And I can get a good education and earn money here at the store at the same time. So, see, I have my fish and my better life." He laughed when he said this, but it wasn't a big laugh.

"It sounds better where you used to live."

Dominique didn't answer me directly. Instead he said, "It will be worth it when I get the scholarship and can go to the university. Then I'll be in one of the best biology programs around, and maybe after that, medical school."

I think Dominique would make a good doctor. I'd rather tell *him* what's hurting me than any other doctor. Dominique takes college courses at the community college, but he says that to get into a good medical school, he needs to go to a good university. And to go to a good university, he needs scholarship money. I hope Dominique gets the money. But then Dominique wouldn't work in the aquarium store anymore, and I'd have to learn about fish from these boring books.

"Gabe? Gabe, honey. It's a beautiful day. Why don't you go outside for a while?"

Instead of answering my mom, I flip through the book and check out the chapter titles: *Cleaning Your Aquarium. Aquarium Landscaping. Water Quality.* How can they make such a cool hobby sound so boring? "I don't want to read this," I say out loud and head downstairs to go outside.

Most of the neighborhood guys are playing soccer in the street in front of our house, as usual. We live in the city—not downtown where the offices and big apartment buildings are, but a few miles away in a neighborhood where the houses are stuck together in rows. Special rules apply to street soccer, mainly to account for the fact that the ball often ends up under one of the cars parked on the street.

My brothers are already out there. Maxie is on Ryan Torrey's team. I see Jake, who seems to be on Ryan's team, too, but it's hard to tell because he's not following the ball so much as he's fiddling around with something he probably took out of the kitchen junk drawer.

Suddenly the ball bounces against Jake's knee. He reacts

way too late, of course, but the ball ricochets over to Ryan, who then kicks it over the chalk-drawn goal line to score.

"Yes!" Ryan exclaims. "Thank you, Jake!"

"Hey, Yo-yo, stop playing with that yo-yo if you want to be on my team!" yells Steven Coombs. So Jake isn't on Ryan's team after all, even though he just helped them score a goal.

"Sorry," Jake says. He puts the yo-yo in this pocket and tries to look like a team player. It's not too hard for him to pull this off. He looks athletic—tan, with strong legs and arms, and humongous hands. I don't know how he holds little bits of charcoal and skinny paintbrushes in those paws when he does his artwork, but he does.

Ha, I think, looking at Jake trying to look like a team player, we'll see how long this lasts. Jake and team sports don't go together. There's too much downtime for him, even in the most action-packed game. I watch as he crouches with his hands on his thighs, as the other kids do, and as he dances up and back, right and left—again, following the ball around the field as the other kids do. But as the ball moves down the street in the control of the other players, Jake loses interest. As I knew he would. As he always does. Not that I can blame him. I find soccer too boring for words and definitely too boring to play.

"Ja-ake!"

That's Steven again. This time Jake accidentally "kicked" the ball out of bounds. He didn't really kick it, since it just kind of bounced off his ankle when he moved his feet. And by a stroke of bad luck, instead of rolling under a car—which doesn't count as out-of-bounds, but is treated as a do-over— the ball managed to bounce through one of the few empty spaces on the street to the sidewalk. So it is truly out-of-bounds, and now Ryan's team gets possession.

"Sorry," Jake says again. "I'm done playing anyway." No one asks him to stay.

I want to yell. I want to push Steven Coombs's face in. I want to give Jake a brain transplant.

Jake seems perfectly okay about leaving the game in disgrace. He comes over to where I'm sitting on the concrete stairs that lead up to the front porch of our house.

"I've figured out how to walk the dog," he says. Before I can ask what dog he's talking about, he takes the yo-yo out of his pocket and does the trick.

"Cool, Jake," I say, meaning it.

"Wanna try?" he asks. Not really, but he hands me the yo-yo without waiting for my answer. He walks toward the curb, right where he bounced the ball out-of-bounds. I see him bend down and pick up one thing, then another, and another. He's pushing his straight dark hair out of his eyes and smiling to himself.

"Whee-yuh!" I hear a scream that sounds familiar. "Whee-yuh! Ah-yah-yah-yah-yah-yah!"

Maxie. He sounds like a dog that's been run over by a car. But I look over at him, and he's all in one short, curly-headed, skinned-knees-and-knuckles piece. All that's happened is that he's blocked Steven's shot, and he's so greatly, hugely, gigantically pleased with himself that he's cheering and laughing as only Maxie can.

"Way to go, kid!" Ryan says. "Hey, Steven, how's it feel to be blocked by a first grader?"

"Whee-yuh!" Maxie is still shrieking.

And I'm thinking: *He's totally crazy.*

I must have said it out loud, because Jake looks over at me and says, "No, he's not. He's happy. He's a first grader who blocked a shot in the sixth-graders' game. Let him celebrate."

I spread my hands out wide, as if to say, *Hey, am I stopping him?*

"Different doesn't mean crazy, Gabe," Jake says.

Easy for you to say, I think. Only, as I watch Jake walk up the stairs into the house, I know that it isn't easy for him to say at all.

Chapter Five

Evan and Me

Two minutes later, I follow Jake back into the house. There, I've been outside in the beautiful day for Mom. Now I can come inside and do what I want to do—play *DeepSea*. Passing through the kitchen on my way to the little computer room, I look on the counter at the stuff from the street that Jake has put there: three bottle caps, an empty matchbox from a restaurant with a picture of a man in a turban on it, and a beat-up penny. I know he'll use them in some art project.

I settle in with old Victor and we make a quick dive, still looking for the *Victoriana*. I know we're not going to find the wreck in this session—I'm going too fast, not feeling up to doing the careful step-by-step stuff necessary to strike gold—but I figure we can map out some new area that will be useful when I'm more focused. After this warm-up, I plan to shift over to a level of the game that I didn't even know existed before last week, when I was talking to Dominique at Tanks for You and found out we both play this game.

Dominique told me how to get to a hidden level. Like most computer games, *DeepSea* has some Easter eggs—special levels you can access if you know the right code. Dominique told me that this hidden level includes a demo of the next game to be released by the company that makes *DeepSea*. That game isn't in the stores yet, but if I enter the cheat code, I can see a preview.

I hear a knock at the front door. I'm closest to it, so I pause the game and hurry to see who it is.

"Hi, Gabe. Whatcha doing?"

"Evan. Hi."

"I saw you come in from the soccer game. I was on my porch."

Evan Peabody lives across the street. We're friends, I guess. No, that's not fair, we are friends. Like me, Evan is no street soccer fan, and he likes computer games. And his mom doesn't make him go outside much. He also likes to fool around with action figures, even though we know that most guys our age have stopped playing with them. It doesn't bother him at all. "It's a lot more fun than running up and down the street chasing a soccer ball," he says. I agree.

So how come I feel disappointed about half the time

when he knocks at my door? Like today. All I want is to go to the hidden level of my game. Without any real-life company.

Mom zips past the front door on her way from the kitchen to the stairs. "Hi, Evan."

"Hi, Anne." In books and on television all the kids seem to call their friends' parents *Mr.* and *Mrs.* Where we live, nearly everyone uses the adults' first names. It's just the way the moms and dads around here introduce themselves to kids.

"You guys are inside?" she asks. Obviously she knows that we, like her, are inside and not outside. What she really means is "I wish you guys would go outside."

"I was already outside," I say. "I want to show Evan something on the computer."

Mom shakes her head, but it's a gentle shake. She worries that I spend too much time by myself, so when I have a friend over she doesn't much care where we hang out. "Is Jake still outside with Maxie?"

"I don't know . . . ," I begin, but then I remember that I followed Jake inside. "No, I think he's inside somewhere."

"Well, then, I'd better check outside on the little guy. I don't want him running into a car." That might seem like a sick joke, but we all know that Maxie is lots better at taking care of himself in the street than either of his older brothers. He sees everything that comes at him, and if he falls or gets hit by a ball or another kid, he just toughs it out or shrugs it off.

"I think Maxie's become an official part of the sixth-graders' soccer team," Evan tells Mom. "He's blocking Steven Coombs's shots."

"Sounds like Maxie," Mom says. "I'll just make sure they're not using him as the ball. Then, Gabe, I'll be up in my room making some calls."

"Okay." When Mom makes a point of telling me that she'll be up in her room making calls, I know they're not calls to chat with friends. She needs to call her clients who leave messages with a special answering service when she's away from her office— which is most of the time when we're home from school. Mom is a social worker, and when we're in school, she meets with clients at an office downtown. They talk. The idea is that by talking about the client's problems, the problems will get better.

I used to wonder why, if Mom is an expert at helping people with problems, she had to take Jake to a doctor to figure out what was wrong with him. Mom explained to me that you can't be a very good doctor or social worker to yourself or to a family member. You're too close to the problem, she said. You won't explore all the possibilities, and you may not be entirely honest about the problem because you don't want to hurt feelings or admit that there may a problem in your own family.

Besides, Mom said, she doesn't treat children.

I think I understand Mom's point about not treating a member of your own family. I guess I can also see why she doesn't want to have children as clients. But I think it's kind of unfair and weird that Mom is an expert at helping people with problems, but she can't be an expert about our problems. When it comes to figuring out Jake's ADHD and LDs and Maxie's goofiness and the fact that I can't seem to get along very well with anybody except Evan and make-believe Victor—and even they aggravate me half the time— well, why does Mom have to punt?

"So, Gabe, what'd you want to show me on the computer?" Evan asks.

I had nothing in mind, actually. I just said that to get Mom off my back.

"Nothing new, really. I was playing *DeepSea Danger Hunt* when you came over. I'm still searching for the *Victoriana*."

Evan groans. "Still? How about we play *Unnatural Force* for a change?"

That's a shoot-'em-up game. You get your choice of twelve kinds of weapons, and you fight against aliens that have weird special powers. They chase you, and you chase them, all around the Earth and across the solar system and beyond. That's where they're from—Beyond. And that's why they have unnatural powers.

I'm tired of shoot-'em-up games. I played them a lot when I was younger—in third and fourth grades—and now Maxie likes them. Come to think of it, he may have gotten his strange soccer shriek—"whee-yuh!"—from the third level of *Unnatural Force* when the Zygurts unleash their pent-up solar energy as they streak through Earth's stratosphere. Suddenly I realize that "whee-yuh!" is almost exactly the sound they make.

"I don't think so," I tell Evan. "That game's boring to me now."

"Come on, Gabe. *DeepSea Danger* is boring to me."

Well, who asked you to come over? I think, but I don't say it out loud. Instead, I sigh, and say, "There's always *Solitaire*."

Evan snorts. "Right, we're gonna play a one-person card game. You would suggest that. Come on. Get real. *Unnatural Force* is about the only game that lets us both play at the same time. Get out the joysticks. It'll be fun."

I give in, and we boot up *Unnatural Force*. Level one: invading Cyrants attack the solar system. But I'm bored, and as defender of the solar system against the Cyrants from Beyond, I'm a total failure. Evan wipes me out in no time.

"Come on, Gabe," he says. "You're supposed to put up a fight."

"Hey, I played the game, didn't I? Sorry if that's not good enough for you."

"Well, let's go to the next level," Evan says. In the second level the Moon is under attack by even more powerful aliens from Beyond—the Tritorgs. I pay more attention this time and manage to hold off annihilation for a while, but finally Evan overpowers me, and the Tritorgs take over the Moon.

"Now my target is Earth itself," Evan says in a sinister voice. "Are you ready, Earth weaklings?" And he presses the key that takes us to the third level. Now, he's the Zygurts, the most fantastically powerful of all the aliens from Beyond.

He puts a fleet of battle stations in orbit around Earth, while I launch missiles in an effort to shoot them down. I miss nearly all my shots and next thing I know Evan is punching the button on his joystick and yelling, "You're toast, Planet Earth!"

"Whee-yuh! Whee-yuh! Whee-yuh!" the computer screeches. "Whee-yuh! Whee-yuh! Whee-yuh!"

"Aah! Stop!" I shout.

"Whee-yuh! Whee-yuh!" every time Evan sends a Zygurt drone from one of his orbiting battle stations down to Earth to explode over a major city. "Whee-yuh! Whee-yuh!"

"Evan!" I yell.

"I know!" he says. "Great battle plan, huh? You are *pulverized*, man!"

"Whee-yuh! Whee-yuh!"

I can't stand it any longer. I know it's bad for the computer. I know it means Evan won't get to see the awesome final explosion when all the major cities on Earth are done for, but I can't listen to this any longer. I push the computer's on/off button. The screeching stops. The game collects itself into a surprised-looking point in the center of the screen. And the screen goes black.

"Hey!" Evan says. "What's your problem?"

"I told you," I say. "I told you to stop!"

"Stop what? Winning?"

"That noise, Evan! That 'whee-yuh, whee-yuh' noise. It was driving me nuts!"

"The Zygurt noise when they stream through the stratosphere?"

I nod. "I hear Maxie doing it all the time. I hate it like crazy!"

Evan looks at me. "Jeez, Gabe," he says. "Why didn't you just turn the sound down?"

I stop, dead still. Then I shake my head. I had forgotten. Why didn't I just turn the sound down?

Evan says he's not mad at me, and I believe him. Things don't shake him up. But he goes home anyway. Now I have the computer to myself, exactly what I wanted all afternoon. Only now I don't feel like playing.

Then I remember there's that hidden level to explore. I turn the computer back on and click on the *DeepSea* icon. When it prompts me to select "New Dive," instead I enter the code Dominique wrote down for me: "FREEZEHOT."

The screen goes blank for a second, and then an underwater landscape appears. There's no introductory screen, no directions. A school of ordinary-looking fish is clustered in the top right-hand corner. There is no diver. I click on the school of fish, and one of them comes to life—that is, I can control it with my mouse.

I move my fish around, and suddenly I'm in a weird environment with strange-looking sea creatures. Unpredictable underwater currents sometimes swirl me away to another part of the environment. An on-screen thermometer indicates that the water temperature changes dramatically depending on where I swim. I come to the rim of what looks like a volcano, and the thermometer goes wild, shooting way, way up. I see other fish disappear in there, but none of them come out. I stay away from the edge.

I swim to a formation on the ocean floor that looks a lot like pictures I've seen of the Grand Canyon, only under water. I move toward the canyon and press CTRL-D, the keyboard combination that lets you make a dive. But I don't move. Instead, the computer beeps twice, then makes these bubble sounds. I notice that the thermometer keeps jumping from thirty-two degrees to two hundred-and-twelve degrees Fahrenheit. It's either freezing cold or boiling hot—or both at the same time?

Congratulations! A message flashes on the screen.

> You've made it to the deepest, coldest part of the ocean. It's so cold here that the water is thick—you can hardly swim. But down deep in the crater, a whole new world exists, where the water vaporizes into steam and a different kind of life form lives. Just how far can you survive? To the earth's core? Don't press CTRL-D to find out, because you can't get there from here! Watch for further releases from DeepDown Software for continued adventures in the deep!

What a rip-off! I press CTRL-D anyway, but nothing happens so I just sit there looking at the underwater Grand Canyon. My fish blows bubbles and hangs above the watery black hole. *Great,* I think, *another letdown. Victor should have warned me about this.*

Chapter Six

Bait-and-Switch

I have now slogged through the *Handbook for the New Aquarist*, and my parents are keeping their promise. It's Saturday, and Dad is taking me to buy an aquarium.

Tanks for You is in a strip of shops on a busy street that's walking distance from our house. Today Dad and I are taking the car, but I've walked over and hung out here lots of times. Besides the fish store, there's a drugstore, small grocery, dry cleaner, ice cream shop, Chinese restaurant, barber, and a sandwich place.

"Hey!" Dominique says when I walk in. "How's it going? I've been expecting you." He smiles. His teeth are very, very white against his dark skin.

"Hi," I say.

"Have you used that cheat I gave you to go to the hidden level in *DeepSea Danger Hunt* yet?"

"Yeah," I say, "a couple days ago. It looks cool!" I don't

tell him how disappointed I was not to be able to explore the deep, dark hole in the sea.

He nods. "I hear the new game will be out in about a month."

I nod back. "Cool," I say again. I feel a little uncomfortable bantering back and forth with Dad around. I mean, I'm just a kid and Dominique's pretty much already a man, but Dominique and I talk a lot. I think Dad might think our conversations are pretty weird and that Dominique's weird for sort of being my friend.

But Dominique doesn't seem in the least uncomfortable. He turns to Dad and says, "I'm Dominique Martin. Gabe and I have been talking for weeks about his new aquarium. We also seem to like some of the same computer games."

"Dominique, I'm Peter Livingston," Dad says. "It's nice to meet you."

"So, Gabe, are you ready to choose your equipment?" Dominique asks, his white teeth flashing.

"Uh—well—sort of."

"Okay. Let's get started setting you up."

I take the list I've made out of my jeans pocket. "Well, a twenty-five-gallon tank," I say. "Acrylic, not glass. A rectangle."

"I don't have to tell you that with acrylic you have to be extra careful not to scratch it, because it shows scratches more than glass," he says.

"Yeah," I answer, "but acrylic tanks look better than glass."

Now Dominique turns to Dad. "Acrylic provides better clarity," he says. "It's also a little more expensive, but not much. He's right to want it." Dad nods his approval, and Dominique disappears into the stockroom to get my acrylic aquarium. When he reappears with the tank in his arms, Dad asks him where he's from.

"Guadeloupe, in the Caribbean. But I've lived here since I was ten years old. Still, we speak a lot of French and Creole at home. So you can hear a little accent in my voice."

"Just a little," Dad says. "And I'd be happy to have an accent if it meant I could speak three languages."

With all the conversations I've had with Dominique, I had not entirely figured out that he speaks with a slight accent. It seemed to me that Dominique just had kind of a musical way of talking.

"Actually, I speak four languages," Dominique says. The smile again when Dad makes an exaggerated surprised face. "Spanish, too. I took it in middle and high school."

Dad nods his appreciation.

"And Dominique takes classes at the community college and is waiting to get a scholarship to the university," I say. "To study biology. And then to go to medical school."

"Well," Dominique says, "I've been admitted to the university. But the only way I can afford to attend is if I get more financial aid than what the school has offered me. So I've applied for this scholarship from a private organization that helps science students. I'm told my chances are good. But I don't know whether the scholarship will come through or not."

"When will you find out?" Dad asks.

"Not until July," Dominique says. He shakes his head. "And it's only May."

"I wish you the best of luck," Dad says.

Dominique gets back to the business at hand. Examining the acrylic tank he brought out from the stock room, he says, "Okay, one brand-new acrylic tank, unscratched as far as I can see. Want to double-check?"

I look it over. Clear as can be. I nod.

"Do you need a stand?"

I shake my head. "No, there's this ledge where it'll fit just right. It's near an outlet so I can plug in the stuff that needs to be plugged in."

"It's not a window seat, is it? You don't want to put an aquarium near a window. The sun will cause algae to grow, and the water can get too hot or too cold."

"Nope, not a window seat. It's a big ledge in the computer room. We used to pile up books and papers and manuals from computer games there. This morning I cleared out the junk that was there."

I tell Dominique all this, and he approves. "So the next items need to be a cover and a light. And a heater and thermometer."

I turn to Dad. "If I only kept cold-water fish, like goldfish, I wouldn't need a heater. But the neatest fish are tropical fish, and they like warm water."

"I can see that this is not your ordinary goldfish bowl," Dad says. "By all means, let's make it comfortable for your new pets."

We add an air pump to keep oxygen circulating in the tank and a filter to help keep the water clean. Then comes colored gravel for the bottom. I choose a combination of neon yellow and orangish-pink.

"Now plants," Dominique says. "Live plants are great, and we have them here—ferns, water sprites, water wisteria. They can help keep the tank clean by reducing the build-up of algae. But I don't recommend them for a beginner, and even lots of experienced aquarists don't use live plants."

"Why not?" Dad asks.

"They're hard to grow and keep alive. They can be particular about their water conditions and sunlight. When they start dying, they can make a real mess in the water. I'd stay away from them."

So I choose a few artificial plants. Then I look at some of the other tank decorations, like large colored stones, little ceramic shipwrecks, and statuettes of deep-sea divers wearing diving suits and helmets.

"Look at this guy," Dominique says when he sees me looking at them. He picked up one of the divers.

"Victor!" I exclaim.

"Sure looks like him, doesn't it?" Dominique says. "But it's just a coincidence. The company that makes this diver has been making him since way before there were computer games."

"Well, maybe one of the programmers at DeepDown Software had one of these guys and modeled Victor after him."

"Could be," Dominique says. "I hadn't thought of that."

"Can I get this diver, Dad?" I ask. "It's not expensive."

Dad checks the price and okays the purchase.

Dominique goes behind the counter to ring everything up. "Okay, we'll add this bottle of water neutralizer, and you'll be all set."

Dad and I look at each other. "Haven't we forgotten something?" I ask.

Dominique looks at all the stuff. "Not unless you want to get a net today," he says. "But that can wait until next time."

I look at him to see if he's joking. But there's no flash of teeth.

"The fish!" I exclaim.

"The fish," Dominique repeats. "Not today. Hey, man, I thought you did your research." Now the teeth flash, but I can tell he's not kidding. "You have to get your aquarium going first, get it all nice and clean and the water all settled and the temperature stabilized. You make a nice home. *Then* you add the fish."

I don't remember reading *that* in that bogus *Handbook for the New Aquarist.*

"Aw, come on!" I say. "This is like bait-and-switch!"

Big grins now from both Dominique and Dad. It takes me a minute to realize that I made a pun—and I didn't mean to. What I meant was that I thought I was getting everything I needed for an aquarium today, and then at the last minute I'm told I can't have the best part.

"I mean," I say as they stand there grinning, "what a rip-off!"

"Come on, Gabe," Dominique says. "I would be ripping you off if I sold you your fish. They'd probably die in a brand-new aquarium."

"You can be patient," Dad says.

I have no choice. Dominique adds up all the equipment and slips a pamphlet on setting up an aquarium in the tank.

Great. Another boring thing to read.

"Thanks, Dad," I say. I know my voice doesn't sound all that grateful, but I really do mean it. We're standing on the sidewalk outside the store.

"You're welcome, Gabe," he says. "Dominique seems to know what he's talking about. I know it's hard to wait, but in a couple of days you'll have your fish."

We load the stuff in the car and then set off on foot to do errands at the drugstore and dry cleaner. Soon it's lunchtime, and we stop in at the sandwich shop to eat.

I like going out to lunch with my Dad. We don't talk all that much, but we have a good time. And we always get a double order of fried onion rings. Mom usually grabs at Dad's stomach if he orders onion rings when she's around, and, as he says, it's hard to enjoy something fully when you've been reminded that it's going to show up right there.

"Let's go home, and you can get to work," Dad says when we step back out on the sidewalk. The car is right in front of the aquarium store. Inside, I can see Mr. Newman, the owner. Dominique just went on his lunch break. We saw him going into the sandwich shop as we came out.

Dad and I stop at the same time. I think we must be having the same thoughts.

"Uh—Can we go in here again?" I ask.

"Well, just for a second," he says. "Yeah," I say.

Mr. Newman is always friendly and agreeable. He agrees, for example, that some fish are hardier than others and that three hardy black mollies and three hardy flame tetras would be a safe way to start off my aquarium. They would look excellent together, too. I should just be careful about getting the temperature right around seventy-five degrees before adding the fish. But that's what I bought a thermometer for, isn't it?

Chapter Seven

Like a Pretzel

Setting up the aquarium is a lot of work. It takes me the whole rest of Saturday. But it's worth it. By Saturday night my aquarium's air pump is humming softly, my artificial ferns are securely planted in the gravel, the water measures a steady seventy-five degrees on my new thermometer, my six hardy new fish are swimming around their new home, and Victor, the little diving man, is anchored among the ferns, watching over this miniature underwater world.

"Good night, guys," I whisper to the fish as I turn out their light before going up to bed. "Good night, Victor." I feel a little silly, but only a little.

Sunday morning I rush downstairs. Mr. Newman knew what he was talking about, right? Still, I'm worried. But I cheer up when I see the six fish swimming just as they had been the night before. Way to go, guys! I feed them—just a little—that's what Mr. Newman and *Handbook for the New*

Aquarist said. One by one the fish wiggle to the surface to gobble a few flakes. They are excellent eaters.

I spend a lot of Sunday watching the fish. I invite Evan to come look at them, and he thinks they're cool. On the computer room floor, we make a giant setup of an underwater battle station, using action figures and all kinds of vehicles and weapons from different action figure sets. The good guys are protecting the endangered species ecosystem, which is the aquarium. They are commanded by me, Jacques Cousteau. The bad guys are trying to invade the ecosystem so they can mine all the uranium-rich gravel, which is worth thousands of dollars per pebble.

It's a terrific game. Of course, we don't touch the tank. Once, when Evan was playing the bad guys, he had one of the action figures tap on the front of the aquarium. I told him that really bothers the fish, and he didn't do it again.

"Good night, guys," I whisper Sunday night. "Thanks for being here." I turn out their light. I no longer feel silly talking to them. I bet Jacques Cousteau talked to fish, too.

~~~   ~~~   ~~~   ~~~   ~~~

Back at school on Monday, before class begins, Sam asks me about my weekend. He's not really a friend of mine, but he's not a bad kid, so I tell him about the new aquarium.

"That sounds cool," Sam says.

"Yeah, it is," I say.

"Really cool," Sam says. "It'd be neat to see."

"Yeah," I say. "Well, anyway. . . ."

Sam nods. "I was at Zach's house last week. He had a new video game he wanted to show me."

Now I nod. And Sam is telling me this because?

"Well, anyway," he says, "if you want to show me your fish someday . . ." and then he trails off.

I'd never thought about inviting Sam over before. Is that what he was getting at? It might be okay. But what would we do?

I worry about things like that. It's one thing to have Evan come over. But what if some new kid came over and wanted just to hang outside the whole time kicking a soccer ball or riding bikes? I know kids who can do that for hours. I'm bored after fifteen minutes. With Evan I know that's okay. With someone new, what if it's not?

By now Sam is organizing his folders for the morning's science and math classes. I don't have to think about this right now. I see Amy Wheeler come in. She usually walks right to her seat, but today, to my surprise, she walks right over and stands in front of me.

"Gabe, did I see you coming out of Tanks for You on Saturday?" she asks.

Her question stumps me for a second. I mean, I don't know whether she saw me or not. On the other hand, I was there so if she thinks she saw me, she probably did.

"You probably did," I say. "I was there with my dad buying stuff to set up an aquarium." And I tell her about my new hobby.

Amazingly, she's interested. "What size tank did you get?" she asks. "Glass or acrylic? Real or fake plants? Salt- or freshwater?" When she sees how shocked I am at her questions, she adds, "Oh, my father keeps a huge aquarium in our living room. It's awesome."

"Oh," I say. Then, not sure what else to say, I ask, "How big is it?"

"A hundred and twenty-five gallons," she says. "It's five feet long."

My eyes must be popping out of my head, because Amy laughs and says, "You'll have to come see it sometime. Dad loves to show it off."

"Okay," I say.

Look how easy it was for Amy Wheeler to invite me over to see her dad's fish. I guess it's perfection like that that makes her part of the Ferris Wheel.

"What does your dad like to show off?" asks Derek. "And why would he want to show it off to Gabie the Baby?" He's just come in and is settling in at his desk, right

57

across from mine.

Amy explains about her father's aquarium while I seethe at Derek's remark.

"And I just got my own aquarium this weekend," I say. "It's not huge, but it's twenty-five gallons. I put six fish in it so far. Black mollies and flame tetras. They're beautiful."

"Beautiful?" Derek says with a laugh. "What fun is beautiful?"

"You already put the fish in?" Amy asks. She's frowning.

I turn to Amy to tell her that my fish are hardy, but what Derek is saying interrupts my train of thought.

"I had a goldfish bowl in second grade," he tells Zach, who's joined our cluster of desks. "It wasn't so beautiful when all the goldfish poop piled up on the bottom." They snicker.

"My cat ate my goldfish," Zach says. "I was in second grade, too. I won the fish at a carnival where you throw ping-pong balls into the little bowls the fish are in. I won two fish that way."

"So, Gabie Baby, now you have a goldfish bowl, too," Derek says. "Well, better late than never. Too bad you're still stuck in second grade." He and Zachary are howling.

I know they're being stupid. I know this is just teasing. But it makes me mad. Before I know it, my desk is crashing into Derek. Then I throw his three-ring binder at his head.

I have such bad aim that I miss his head, but the three rings pop open and Derek's papers scatter across the floor.

"Idiot!" he yells at me.

"You're the idiot!" I yell back. Five minutes later we're in Mrs. Mead's office.

"And we haven't even said the Pledge of Allegiance yet," she says, shaking her head in disapproval. "You boys will have to sit and wait. I have other things to take care of before I find out why you're here so early in the morning."

We sit, Derek and I, in the trouble chairs outside Mrs. Mead's door. But she's not in her private office. Instead, she's busy in the outer office where the secretary sits and where the teachers' mailboxes are. She reviews the morning song and announcements with the three kids who are in charge of them this morning. When she's satisfied that everything is on track, she pushes the button that turns on the public address system and hands the microphone to Miguel Ruiz, a third grader.

"Good morning," he begins. He stops when he hears his voice echoing in the hallway outside. Then he grins widely—it is cool to hear your voice over the public address system—and continues. "Today is Monday . . ."

After Miguel makes a few announcements, the second kid recites the Pledge. Then the third kid introduces this morning's song, "This Land is Your Land,"—*who chose that?*

I wonder—which plays for about fifteen seconds on a boom box with the microphone held up to it. Finally, the trio hand the microphone over to Mrs. Mead.

"Thank you, Miguel Ruiz, Ellie Jamison, and Cory Stadler. Now, boys and girls, I have Hugs to announce—"

Hugs again. Hugs for someone else.

"Congratulations to Derek Dempsey. This morning Derek turned in three comic books that he found on the playground after school last Friday. Thank you, Derek."

Mrs. Mead looks right at Derek sitting next to me in a trouble chair and raises her eyebrows as if to say, *So this is how a HUGS student behaves?*

I sigh so loud that Mrs. Mead shoots me a look, too. The look I get is different from the look Derek got. The look I get is, *Another Monday, another problem with Gabe Livingston.* At least that's how her look looks to me.

Then it sinks into my brain how Derek earned his Hug. He found comic books on the playground and turned them in! Just like I did! And Derek took the comic books home over the weekend. He got to read and re-read them. I didn't do that when I did my comic book good deed in the pre-Hugs days.

I sigh loudly again. Derek pulls his body away. "What're you trying to do?" he mutters. "Pollute the whole room with your breath?"

"Shut up," I mutter back. "It's already polluted because you're sitting here."

"Ouch!" he says. "I'm gonna cry."

Ms. Gamboling, the secretary, looks up from her desk and scowls. "Quiet," she commands. Mrs. Mead is now in her private office, but she's not ready for us yet.

"Gabe!" I hear a voice that sounds way too happy under the circumstances. "Hi, Gabe! Why are you here?"

It's Maxie. "I'm just here, Maxie," I say. "I'm not supposed to talk to you right now."

"Maxie, what brings you here?" asks Ms. Gamboling. "Are you delivering your class's lunch money?"

Maxie shakes his head. "Ms. Carroll isn't done collecting it yet."

"Did she send you to the office?"

Maxie nods. "I'm supposed to talk to Mrs. Mead."

I hear Mrs. Mead finish the telephone call she's been on. She comes out of her office. "What are you supposed to talk to me about, Maxie?"

"About sitting like a pretzel in the rug area," he says.

"About sitting like a pretzel," Mrs. Mead repeats.

"In the rug area," Maxie says.

"Ms. Carroll wants you to sit like a pretzel when you're in the rug area, is that it?" Mrs. Mead says.

"Yes," says Maxie.

"Can you show me how you sit like a pretzel?"

Maxie looks around. "Right here?"

"Right here," says Mrs. Mead.

Maxie sits down on the floor near my chair. He crosses his legs in front of him to form a sort of lap. Then he looks up at Mrs. Mead.

"And were you not sitting like this in the rug area this morning while Ms. Carroll was trying to collect the lunch money?" Mrs. Mead asks.

"I was," says Maxie. "Only then it got hard, so I stopped."

"It got hard?"

"Yeah—my legs got tired."

"Your legs got tired just sitting there on the floor?" A few seconds ago Mrs. Mead looked sympathetic, but now she's beginning to look aggravated.

"Mrs. Mead," I say. "I don't want to interrupt, but—"

"But you are," she says.

"It's about what Maxie is saying," I continue, even though I know she's not happy with me. "I think he means his legs fell asleep. That's what he means when he says his legs got tired."

"That's what I mean!" Maxie exclaims. "They got sleepy and prickly so I had to uncross them."

Mrs. Mead's aggravation seems to be changing into

something else. "Oh! So your legs fell asleep. And what did you do then?"

"I sat regular—like this," and Maxie sticks his legs out in front of him. He's not big, and they're not long legs, but unfortunately at just this moment Ms. Carroll walks into the office. She doesn't seem to notice that there's a kid sitting on the floor.

"Oh!" cries Ms. Carroll as she trips over Maxie's legs. She catches herself, but only after she hops thuddingly to stop the fall. Derek snickers, but quickly catches himself. Looking down, Ms. Carroll finally sees Maxie—and boy, is she steaming!

"Max Livingston!"

"Max was just telling me about his problem in the rug area," Mrs. Mead says. I could be wrong, but it looks to me as if she is working to keep from smiling.

"Yes! He needs to sit like a pretzel," Ms. Carroll says. "There are twenty-five children in the class. If everyone just decided they couldn't sit like a pretzel . . ." Her voice keeps rising, "Just imagine! They'd be flipping all over each other!"

"Do you understand what Ms. Carroll is saying, Maxie?" Mrs. Mead asks. "What would happen if everyone stopped sitting like a pretzel?"

Maxie thinks. "Our legs would all wake up?"

Now there's no question about it. Mrs. Mead is definitely

tightening her mouth to keep from smiling. "And what else?" she asks.

He thinks some more. "I know!" he says in the excited voice he uses when he knows the answer to something. "We all couldn't fit on the rug!"

Mrs. Mead reaches down to help Maxie get to his feet. "Try to sit like a pretzel in the rug area," she says. "If your legs are falling asleep, see if it helps to shake them a little while they're crossed. Or raise your hand to tell Ms. Carroll."

Maxie looks like he wants to say something, but Mrs. Mead puts her finger on her lips and shakes her head. "Ms. Carroll, I think Maxie is ready to rejoin the class now," she says. Mrs. Mead smiles at Maxie and gives him an encouraging pat on the shoulder. She gives Ms. Carroll a displeased look. I think Mrs. Mead is still trying to figure out why Maxie was sent to the office.

Now it's Derek's and my turn.

"What happened?" Mrs. Mead asks us.

"He can't take a joke!" Derek begins, always first to explain, always ready with a theory of what's wrong with me. This time, I don't even listen. I answer Mrs. Mead's questions with half my brain; the other is back in the classroom, remembering Amy Wheeler's worried look when I said I already had fish in my new aquarium. Mrs. Mead gives us both notes that our parents have to sign.

We're walking out the door when Mrs. Mead calls me back. Again. She talks to me about calming down, not being so hard on everyone, not being so hard on myself. Just focus on my schoolwork. Maybe if I didn't expect to find fights and insults everywhere, they wouldn't happen. "You need to work on letting things go, Gabe," she says. "Just calm down when you get into situations with the other kids."

Easy for her to say. Nobody called her an idiot today.

"When you sense a conflict with other kids brewing," Mrs. Mead continues, "step back. Disengage. Float above it." She smiles what I suppose is meant to be an encouraging smile.

"I don't know," I say. "I think I'm more into diving below than floating above."

The smile disappears. It suddenly occurs to me that what I just said could be viewed as a smart-alecky answer.

"Okay, Gabe," Mrs. Mead says. There's no smiling in her voice; she's back to all business. "Maybe that's what you need to work on—diving below trouble. You can go back to your classroom now."

But wait! I want to say. *All I meant was . . .* I'm not sure what I meant.

Maybe diving below and floating above are about the

same thing. Maybe if I just dove below the waves churned up by people like Derek, I'd be better off. The good thing is I wouldn't be splashing around on the surface and getting in trouble. The bad thing is I'd be submerged, alone, and I feel like that already. A lot.

Chapter Eight

Albert Einstein and Me

After school, I give Mom the note from Mrs. Mead, and she gives me one of those worried looks.

"This makes two incidents in less than a week," she says. "What's going on, Gabe?"

As if I knew. "I just can't get along with other kids," I say. "They always bother me."

"Always? I saw Evan Peabody and you getting along just fine over the weekend and after school last week."

"That's just Evan," I say.

"Well, why doesn't he count?" Mom asks. "Why do you think you can get along with him but not anybody else?"

Jake walks in about then, and I really don't want to have this conversation in front of anybody, even Jake. Besides,

I'm tired of answering questions.

"Mom, do we have to talk about this now? I'd just like to have a snack in peace, if you don't mind." I've taken my usual—a few slices of American cheese, a heap of little gold-fish-shaped crackers, and a bunch of green grapes. I might top it off with a chocolate-chip granola bar or two.

"I do mind," Mom says, "but we don't have to do this now." She looks like she wants to have that talk right now. But I'm happy to take her at her word. She hands Jake a piece of paper with his psychiatrist's name at the top.

"Jake, you have a doctor's appointment tomorrow at lunchtime, remember," she says. "So I'll pick you up from school at eleven-fifteen."

Jake nods. Then I hear the sound of flushing water from the hall bathroom, and Maxie comes in the kitchen, drying his hands on his pants.

"I'm glad you remembered to wash your hands," Mom says to him. "Next time use the towel."

"Did Gabe tell you about seeing me in the office this morning?" Maxie asks. He seems almost proud.

"No, Maxie," I say. "I don't tattle."

"I wouldn't care if you told," he says to me. Then, to Mom: "Ms. Carroll sent me to the office for not sitting like a pretzel in the rug area."

Mom's mouth starts to work the same way Mrs. Mead's

did. Lucky Maxie. He'll get the whole story out, Mom will think it's no big deal, and then he'll go play like nothing happened. Maybe he's not crazy after all. I, on the other hand, can look forward to major conversations with Mom and Dad about "What's Going on at School."

I'm starting to think that Jake's lucky, too, like Maxie. His problems are fixed by taking pills. If he acts different, it has a reason: ADHD. He never seems to have to "float above" anything. He collects his street junk and turns it into art and doesn't fight with the kids who say he's stupid and clumsy. Is he too stupid to care or notice? Or is he too smart?

I wonder if they make a pill that would make me calm down, let things go, not be so hard on other people . . . and otherwise improve my soccer game, clean up my room, and, hey, why not contribute to world peace while we're at it? Actually, I couldn't care less about soccer. My room is neat enough. And I don't know why I should joke about world peace. It's not any more likely to break out soon than I am likely to float above problems.

"I'm going up to make my phone calls," Mom says. Maxie is gone. A sprinkling of orange cracker crumbs marks his place at the table. Jake is sifting through the stuff in his kitchen junk drawer, a place that Mom has set aside for his collectibles. "Maybe you and I can talk more in about half an hour, Gabe."

I shrug. After I hear her running upstairs to her bedroom—Mom never walks the stairs, she always runs—I take the flipbook I made during recess out of my back pocket.

As I flip from back to front, I see a boy who looks amazingly like Derek Dempsey fall into a huge goldfish bowl and drown a very bubbly death, after which his corpse is gobbled up in one bite by a giant goldfish. On the last page I also drew in a speech balloon next to the goldfish that says: "Hugs to you, Derek!"

I decide to pass on the granola bars and take my dish to the sink. Mom has left her briefcase on the kitchen counter. It's small and made of leather—like a large cowhide envelope. Mom usually leaves it unzipped so she can fit more stuff in. There's usually a psychology or social work book of some sort spilling out of it, and today is no exception. *Your Difficult Child* is the title of this one.

But Mom doesn't treat children.

Who's a difficult child? I wonder. I start reading the inside flap of the cover.

> Our children can be different in many ways—many ways that deviate from the norm, the average, the kid next door. One child may be different physically; perhaps she is strikingly beautiful, or unusually tall. Another child's difference may be his mental abilities; he may have a learning disorder that hinders his ability to read

or solve math problems. The list of differences is as long and varied as human characteristics. This book is about a difference in temperament—what you might also call mood. This book is about the Difficult Child.

Who's a Difficult Child? I ask myself again. And I wonder: Is there really a whole book written all about kids in bad moods by a man whose name begins with Doctor? I open the book and start reading.

Who is a Difficult Child? He is not the child who falls into a bad mood from time to time. The Difficult Child has an in-born temperament that seems to cause him to hit more rough spots on the road of Life than the average person. This temperament may cause the child to be easily irritated, both by people and by environment. For example, many difficult children find certain types of clothing intolerably itchy or uncomfortable. The same in-born temperament can lead to moodiness, wherein the child seems to pull into himself and away from others and is given to feelings of sadness. The Difficult Child may experience her wants, likes, and dislikes with great intensity, and as a result may appear to be unreasonably rigid, demanding, or opinionated. The Difficult Child has trouble adapting to the unexpected and tends to take disappointments hard.

People who don't really know our Difficult Child may attach labels to him but, like most labels, these may do more harm than good. For example, a Difficult

Child who is very easily distracted may be labeled "hyper," suggesting the hyperactivity that accompanies Attention Deficit Hyperactivity Disorder. But the Difficult Child is not necessarily the ADHD child. The Difficult Child's distractibility is more likely to stem from his wide-ranging imagination than from his inability to stay on task. Similarly, a Difficult Child may be called "high-strung," as if she is simply a case of tightly wound nerves. But what the observer may see as mere high-strung nervousness is actually evidence of the Difficult Child's intense curiosity. She is not so much "nervous" as she is deeply, intensely involved in her world.

Is this me? Is Mom reading a book so she can figure me out? I feel my pulse beating like crazy, right behind my eyes. This is like reading a thriller, a mystery.

Does this prove that I'm crazy? Is this book about me?

I re-read the part about being called "high-strung." No one's ever called me that to my face, that's for sure. But maybe in kindergarten, overhearing the conference between Mom and the teacher . . . I don't really remember, but it sounds kind of familiar.

This book is about me.

I'm still standing over the kitchen counter with Mom's book when I hear her footsteps on the stairs.

"You're still here!" she says, surprised.

I hold up the book. "What kind of a book is this?" I ask.

"What were you doing in my briefcase?" she asks back.

"I wasn't in your briefcase," I say. "Your briefcase was open right here on the counter, and I saw this when I came to put my dishes in the sink. Who's a Difficult Child? Is it me?"

Mom takes the book and her little briefcase and sits down at the table. I follow.

"Is it me?" I ask again. "I thought you said it's a bad idea to treat your own children."

Mom flips through the book before answering. "I'm not treating my own children," she says. "I'm not treating you. I don't think you need treating. And actually, Dad saw this book in a bookstore, and he bought it and read it. He gave it to me, and now I'm reading it."

"But you're not reading it just for fun," I say. "Is it me? Am I the Difficult Child?"

Mom runs her hand through her hair. "I don't care much for labels," she says. "Sometimes we're all difficult children, including adults. Were we thinking of you when we saw this book? Yes. Are you a Difficult Child as defined in this book? I don't know. It doesn't really matter. I don't think you're such a difficult person or child, but I know you're having some difficulty at school and with other kids. I know you have a short fuse on your temper sometimes and you can be impatient."

I think about my rush to get the fish into my aquarium. Ouch.

"So, according to this book, I'm a Difficult Child. So now what? Does this doctor say there's a pill for it? Do I go to special classes?"

I don't know why I'm mad at Mom. After all, the parts of the book I was reading didn't make the Difficult Child sound like such a terrible person. This doctor even sounded as if he liked Difficult Children.

"I'm not saying you're anything. You're not going to force me to put a label on you, and you shouldn't label yourself either. This book is saying that we all have certain personalities that we're just born with, and one type of personality is—"

"Is *difficult!*" I interrupt her. "So if you're difficult, that's just tough luck. You just have to live with it, with everyone hating you and you hating everyone else, too!" I stand up because I'm so mad I can't sit still anymore.

Mom holds up her hand. "*Difficult* is just another label. This book isn't interesting because it attaches a label to certain people. It's interesting because of what it says is going on inside certain people, maybe even you. It's interesting because it says that some kids have a hard time getting along not because they're bad or mean and nasty or stupid or anti-social. They're intense and observant and smart and creative and not willing to just go with the flow—they're individuals. Sometimes that can make life hard for those kids, because the people around them demand conformity and smooth edges. But it also makes these kids wonderful."

Mom's words have been coming out in a big rush. I'm almost afraid she's going to cry. But she doesn't. She takes a breath and asks, "Does this help you at all?"

"Yeah—I'm wonderful. And Jake, he's so totally not interested in going with the flow that he's off the wonderfulness chart. Maxie, well, he's too young to tell."

Mom purses her lips. "We're talking about you, not Jake or Maxie. Look, maybe you don't want to hear words like 'you're wonderful.' You have a terrific imagination, and you seem to think and feel deeply about things. Those are wonderful qualities. If some edginess comes with those qualities, so be it. You'll learn to live with it, and so will the people around you."

Edginess. Now there's a word. Not difficult, not easy, not good or bad. I see myself balancing on an edge—a fence, a rim, a cliff, a rail. On the edge of the deep, dark underwater canyon. Edges don't scare me. They seem to get my juices going.

"I can live with edginess," I say, meaning to sound light and funny, but it comes out dead serious.

"I think you can, too," says Mom. She pushes the book toward me. "Since you've already read part of this, you may as well have a look at the chapter about some real-life difficult children. I think you'll recognize their names."

I look at the page Mom has open and start reading.

Pablo Picasso. Winston Churchill. Thomas Alva Edison. Albert Einstein. A great artist, statesman, inventor, scientist—and each one a Difficult Child. Winston Churchill, for example, was uncoordinated, badly behaved, and hyperactive as a schoolboy. He grew up to become one of the most insightful, energetic, and focused statesman of modern time. But he didn't leave his so-called "difficult" side behind entirely. Even as an adult, he could be moody and edgy. He also held onto a child-like love of silly songs and play.

I look up to see if Mom is reading what I'm reading. She's nodding. "I know," she says. "Gabe, people are complicated. Life can be complicated. And I mean that in a wonderful way."

Picasso. Churchill. Edison. Einstein.

Einstein! I have to remember this page next time Derek yells, "Hey, Einstein!" in my face. There definitely are worse insults.

Not that I think I'm going to be the next Albert Einstein or anything. I wonder if Jacques Cousteau was difficult. . . .

Chapter Nine

Fish Are a Little Like People

My fish are dead. First one black molly went belly up, and then the other two later that same day. The next morning I found the flame tetras floating lifeless, mid-tank, all three of them.

It's my fault. I knew that Mr. Newman was just crossing his fingers for me when he sold Dad and me the fish before I had set up my aquarium. Now it's just Victor in the tank.

So I've started over. The fish went down the toilet, along with the water in the aquarium. I washed the gravel, re-anchored the plants, and gave Victor a new place to stand. I added fresh water and treated it with special drops, using the instructions in my new Bible, *Handbook for the New Aquarist*. The water turned cloudy at first, but then cleared up fine—just like the book said it would. The temperature has been around seventy-five degrees Fahrenheit for five days. This aquarium is ready for fish.

It's Saturday, and Dad drops me off at Tanks for You while he takes care of some errands. "Is half an hour too long?" he asks before we go our separate ways.

"No. Don't hurry," I say. I could use an hour in the store. I'm going to take my time because I'm doing things right this time. I hope Mr. Newman isn't here. I think we'd both be embarrassed if I had to tell him that the fish died.

"Hey, Gabe!" Dominique greets me. "I know you're careful, buddy, but you didn't have to wait this long to get your fish!"

It's been three weeks since I bought my aquarium. Dominique doesn't know what I did, and I guess I don't have to tell him, but I confess anyway. If he's disappointed, he doesn't show it.

"Yeah," he says as he nods slowly, "fish'll die on you. It happens to us all." He pops his chewing gum, which I've noticed he seems to do when he's thinking. "Did they have white spots when they died?"

I try to remember. "I don't know," I admit.

"Maybe they had icky," he says—or at least that's what I think he says.

I laugh. "Maybe they were icky?"

Now Dominique flashes his teeth. "No, man, fish are

never icky, not to me. Maybe they had ichthyo. It's a very common fish disease. They get white spots."

I try to remember again. "I don't think they had spots."

"Overfeeding?"

"Nah," I say. I know enough not to overfeed fish. I never gave the mollies and tetras more than they could eat in two or three minutes. I'm pretty sure there wasn't any uneaten, decaying food polluting my tank.

"Hmm," Dominique says. "Well, sometimes you just don't know."

"I guess the tank wasn't ready," I say.

"Could be," he says. "It's a little ecosystem, and it can be delicate."

I nod. Don't I know it.

"But it's ready now?" Dominique asks.

"It's really ready," I say. "And I think I'd like something more interesting than black mollies and flame tetras. I just got those the first time because they're supposed to be hardy."

"Something more interesting?" Dominique is walking down the aisle looking into the display tanks that hold fish that are for sale.

"Like a clown loach," I say. "They're kind of goofy-looking, but it might be fun to have one. And a couple of Siamese fighting fish would be cool. And, well, I like angelfish, and the blue gourami is a good fish." I'm walking among the display tanks, too, as I talk.

"They're all good fish," Dominique agrees. "But, you know, fish are a little like people. You can't just throw them together and expect everyone to get along."

Now I remember some of the pointers in my handbook. "Oh, right," I say, "I can't have a pair of Siamese fighting fish. They could kill each other."

"But you can have one," Dominique says, "and it will leave other types of fish alone."

And clown loaches, I remember, like company. A single clown loach might actually die of loneliness.

"And you have to think about traffic patterns, too," Dominique adds. "The clown loaches like the bottom part of the tank, and angels hang out in the middle. Tetras like the middle, too, and they're small so they might look nice in there with a few angels. Try a different type of tetra this time."

I settle on two large angelfish, two clown loaches, six head-and-tail-light tetras, and a sucker-mouth catfish, which will scavenge for food on the bottom of the tank and help keep the aquarium clean. The angelfish are white and light purple with black stripes, very tall and not very long. The clown loaches are orange with black rings around their bodies and over their eyes, which make them look like clowns. Bright yellow spots on the tetras give them their name, head-and-tail-light. I think these eleven fish will make a fine community. For now, I decide to pass on the Siamese fighting fish.

While Dominique and I are gently putting the fish in plastic bags for their ride home, the door opens and a customer comes in.

"Mr. Wheeler!" Dominique calls. "How's the reef tank?"

It's Amy Wheeler's father. "Always a challenge, Dominique," he answers.

I've heard about reef tanks. They're saltwater aquariums for corals, which are tiny animals that build rock-like reefs with their skeletons. Reef tanks are kind of complicated to set up and keep going. They're for real experts.

"Hi, Gabe," a familiar voice says.

I look toward the door. It's Amy, who has just walked in to join her father.

"Hi, Amy," I say. "Here with your Dad?" *No, idiot*, I say to myself. *She's here with Albert Einstein.*

But Amy just says, "Yup. He needs some kind of doodad for his tank."

"The reef tank," I say.

"No, the other one," Amy says. "He has another saltwater tank, the one with fish."

"Yeah, Gabe, Mr. Wheeler's marine tank," Dominique says. "It's fantastic."

Mr. Wheeler looks pleased.

"The colors are so intense," Dominique continues. "He's got a purple tang, Picasso triggerfish, a blue devil damselfish. They really stand out."

"Don't forget the copper-banded butterfly fish," Amy adds.

"Or my green parrot wrasse," Mr. Wheeler says. "Can you tell, Gabe, that this aquarium is my pride and joy?"

I nod.

"Kind of silly for a grown man, you think?"

I shake my head.

"It's not silly," Amy says.

"Every so often we have to buck up Mr. Wheeler about his hobby," Dominique says to me. "I think whenever he's about to spend some more money on it, he starts feeling sheepish."

"It's a work of art, Dad," Amy says, "and an ongoing scientific experiment."

"Not everyone can see it that way," I say, thinking of a couple of my classmates.

"So?" Amy says.

"You're exactly right, Gabe," Mr. Wheeler says. "My wife is among those without our vision." He laughs. "Any word on the scholarship, Dominique?"

"Not yet," Dominique answers. "It'll be a few more

weeks before I hear."

"Tough to wait, I bet," Mr. Wheeler says.

"I'm trying not to think about it. I mean, I like working here, and the classes I take at the community college are good. But to be able to focus full-time on school would be so . . ." He pauses, searching for the right word. ". . . so *fine*. And the university's biology programs have such a good reputation. I'd love to be there."

You can tell how much Dominique wants it. He gazes off, eyes half-closed, like he doesn't want to look directly at his dream because if he does he'll jinx it.

Mr. Wheeler buys the doodad he needs for his marine tank, and then he and Amy leave. I'm ready with my plastic bags of fish, just waiting for Dad to pick me up, when the door opens again.

"Hey, Dom-Dom-Dominique," says the big man who walks in.

"Hey, Tom-Tom-Thomas," Dominique says. He flashes his smile. The big man doesn't smile back. He walks directly to the display tanks and stares at them as if he's looking for something.

"There's not much new since last time," Dominique tells him.

"No new purples?" the big man asks.

"Nope," Dominique says. "But check out the black-and-white fish in the tank in the corner."

Thomas plants himself in front of the aquarium Dominique has pointed out. For a minute, Dominique and I stand and watch the big man watch the fish.

I know this man, Thomas Doherty. It's kind of hard to miss him if you pass him on the street. He's big, with clumsy-looking hands, a big stomach that sticks out over his skinny legs, and brown hair that he wears in a crew cut. He always wears the same outfit—khaki pants and a white collared shirt, long-sleeved in cold weather, short-sleeved when it's warm. Thomas is a regular at almost all of the shops in this strip. Lots of people call him Tom-Tom, because that's what he tells you to call him—if he bothers to talk to you at all. I call him Thomas. It doesn't feel right calling a grown man Tom-Tom.

But Thomas isn't your average, everyday grown-up. Something is wrong with his brain, so he's not as smart as a grown-up should be, or even as smart as a kid in sixth grade. Thomas doesn't act very happy, but he also doesn't act very sad—mainly he seems kind of blank. I wonder how that would feel. In some ways, I think it would be good, but I don't know.

Dominique says that Thomas has feelings just like everyone else, he just doesn't show them the same way. You can tell Thomas is happy, Dominique says, when he hums. I've heard Thomas hum, always songs that I don't recognize, but he doesn't smile or otherwise look cheerful when he hums. He just hums. When he's unhappy, Dominique says, Thomas clicks his tongue against his teeth, or he blinks a lot.

Today Thomas is just staring at the fish, not humming or clicking or blinking.

"Thomas, I've been thinking. I'd like to do something," Dominique says, "if it's all right with you."

"What, Dom-Dom? What do you want to do?" Thomas doesn't take his eyes off the tank.

"I'd like to make you a nice aquarium that you can have at home," Dominique says. "You can have fish living in your apartment."

Now Thomas turns around. "That would be beautiful," he says. "I can have colorful fish?"

"Definitely," Dominique says.

"But I don't have the money to pay for them," Thomas says. "And my sister—I don't want to ask her for the money."

Thomas lives in one of the three-story apartment buildings down the street from the shopping strip. Dominique told me that Thomas eats breakfast and lunch in his apartment, but for dinner he goes to his sister's house. He takes the city bus because she lives a few miles away.

"You don't have to pay," Dominique says. "Mr. Newman said you can have it for free because you sometimes go and get us lunch. You do us favors, so we'll do you this favor."

"I would love that favor," Thomas says. "When will you do it for me?"

"I'll start planning the aquarium right away," Dominique says.

"I could help," I offer.

"Great," Dominique says. "And we can set it up in Thomas's apartment next week. Does that sound okay, Thomas?"

"That sounds . . . beautiful," Thomas says. "Especially if there are purples."

I feel a little bad, because I think Thomas is talking about angelfish when he mentions "purples," and the last two purple-and-white angelfish in the store are in a plastic bag coming home with me.

"On Monday," Dominique says, "we'll be getting in new angelfish. So you'll have your purple fish, Thomas."

Thomas clasps his hands together and turns to look at Dominique and me directly for the first time since he's entered the store. "That will be beautiful," he says. "Thank you." He turns around to look at the tanks again, but doesn't seem to want to stand still anymore. "Well—good luck," he blurts out, spinning around to look at us again. "Good-bye." He leaves the store, humming.

"'Good luck'?" I repeat to Dominique.

He smiles, nodding. "Sure," he says. "Thomas has seen plenty of customers come and go with fish that start out alive and end up dead. He knows how hard it is to make a really nice aquarium work. He knows we could use some luck if he's going to get a good aquarium."

Just then my Dad walks in the store.

"How about Tuesday for setting up Thomas's aquarium?" Dominique asks as we're leaving. "After school?"

Now that Dad's here, I'm in a hurry to get my new fish home. "Tuesday is fine," I say. "Wish me luck."

Chapter Ten

Maxie and Me

I take my time introducing the fish to their new home. I float their plastic bags in the aquarium water, until the water temperature in the tank and the temperature in the bags are the same. Then I open the angelfish bag and let the fish swim out, which they do slowly, as if in a daze. I don't think there's anything wrong with them. I think that's just the way angelfish are. The clown loaches are next, then the six tetras, which practically burst out of the bag and frantically race to the four corners of the tank. Finally I release the sucker-mouth catfish, which sinks to the bottom and begins his careful exploration of the gravel.

"Good night, fish," I whisper as I turn out their light. "Stay healthy."

Sunday morning I check on the aquarium. Victor is standing watch, and the fish are moving, looking good. I turn on the light, sprinkle some food on the water's surface, and watch the fish rush to get their share of breakfast. The book says that an excellent appetite is a sign of health. I think I've got things off to a good start this time.

The aquarium hums softly as the pump pulls water through the filter and bubbles it out the tube. I think of Thomas Doherty humming. Is he actually happy when he hums, or just in a zone? Maxie hums, too. I guess you could say he hums when he's happy, but I really think the humming is more like breathing. He does it when he's doing something else, like coloring or playing with his little toy cars. He doesn't do it when he's upset. Why am I thinking about Maxie and Thomas together?

Well, why not? And who knows, maybe if I started humming and screaming "whee-yuh!" every so often I wouldn't be so *difficult*. Maybe when Thomas has a humming aquarium of his own, he won't click so much.

~~~ ~~~ ~~~ ~~~ ~~~

Monday morning, early, I hear Dad in the kitchen when I'm in the computer room. I've fed the fish and noticed that their color and activity haven't decreased since they've moved in. That's a good sign. I think my last family of fish was already sluggish and starting to look pale by Monday morning. Now I'm listening to the aquarium filter hum while I'm playing *Unnatural Force* on the computer. Although I usually think this game is boring, early in the morning when I'm too sleepy to think and strategize (the way I have to for *DeepSea Danger Hunt*), fighting invading Zygurts from Beyond is just the thing to get my juices going. But I remember to turn the sound down this time.

I've done a better job than usual defending the solar system against the Cyrants, and before I know it, I'm on the third level, defending the Earth. I've sent up Stealth Satellites, which are feeding me tons of information about the Zygurt battle stations. Whenever I have enough information to pinpoint a battle station's location, I launch a missile and *tzow!* it's blown away. If I win this level, I'll finally get to the fourth and fifth levels, where I actually travel to the Beyond to fight the Cyrants, Tritorgs, and Zygurts in their home territory. I've never seen the Beyond.

"Good morning, Gabe," Dad calls from the kitchen.

"Morning" is all I manage. I'm concentrating, miles away from the sleepy condition I was in just ten minutes ago.

"Want to take a break and have something to eat with me?" he asks. "I've made cinnamon toast."

I love cinnamon toast. Dad makes it the right way, too. First he mixes together sugar and cinnamon, then he butters the bread, then he sprinkles on the cinnamon sugar mixture, and finally he broils the bread in the oven. It takes a few minutes, but it's worth the wait.

I pause the game and join my dad at the kitchen table. He's reading the sports section of the paper. I take two slices of cinnamon toast from the broiler pan. I eat a bite of one, realize I'm thirsty, and get up to pour a glass of milk. I stumble over my shoelace as I'm walking back to the table and almost spill it. "Jeez!" I exclaim. My chair scrapes the floor as I sit down again. I cut one of the pieces of toast in half, and the knife clatters on the table. I'm a big klutz this morning for some reason.

Dad never looks up once. This is how it is with him. He likes company for breakfast, but that's really all he wants— company. Not conversation. He talks all day at work, he says. At breakfast I think he only wants another body at the table.

It's fine with me. I like to look at the weather page in our local newspaper. I check out high and low ocean tides, even though the beach is three hours away. Chewing and gulping and rustling are our morning sounds. I don't understand people—like Maxie and Mom—who carry on entire conversations at the breakfast table. How can there be so much to say when the day is just beginning?

A big paper rustle stirs the air as Dad folds the sports section back to its original condition. "Well, it's that time again," he says, meaning it's time for him to go to work. He likes to be at the office early. I wait for the sound of his chair pushing back from the table, but it doesn't happen. Something in the paper must have caught his eye.

I look over at Dad and am surprised to see him looking not at the newspaper but at me.

"What?" I say. "What is it?"

He shakes his head as if he's decided not to say something he was going to say. But then he leans forward to say it. "Try to get the week off to a good start, Gabe," he says. "I mean, at school. If one of those kids who ruffles your feathers says something annoying, just walk away. Rise above it. Can you do that?"

Here we are having a perfectly nice breakfast, and Dad has to bring this stuff up. There it is again—*rise above it . . . float above it*—as if I'm supposed to imitate some kind of dead fish. *Ruffle your feathers*. What am I, a bird? Or some kind of weird bird-boy-fish combination with feathers to ruffle and legs to walk away on and fins to float above things with.

"Sure, Dad," I say. "I'll walk, fly, and float away. Whatever. Derek and Zach and the rest of them can say anything they want, and I'll just zone out. I'll be just like Jake."

"You know that's not what—" Dad begins. But he interrupts himself. "Being like Jake would not be a terrible thing," he says instead. "But you're a different person. I just want you to be you. "Listen," Dad changes the subject. "The Bermuda program at work has been extended through the end of June. If a few new accounts come through for me—a few big, new customers—we just may win that vacation. How would you like that?" Dad's been trying to qualify for a free vacation that his company is offering if he sells a ton of office machines and stuff.

"I'd like it," I say. "You know I'm dying to learn how to snorkel. Maybe I can learn how to float above things in Bermuda."

Dad gives me a look, a pat on the top of my head, and then he's gone.

Back in the computer room, I rejoin the world of *Unnatural Force* and resume the battle against the invading Zygurts. Now that I'm fully awake, the game is starting to bore me. Send up a Stealth Satellite; shoot down a Zygurt battle station. Look out for the Zygurt drones launched from their battle stations; try to intercept them with missiles. It's all so simple. I could play this game with my eyes shut.

So that's what I do. I squeeze my eyes closed and play by feel and sound and instinct, randomly sending up satellites and missiles. I hear the sound of a Zygurt battle station exploding. Yeah, I can play this game with my eyes shut. I click the joystick buttons in random patterns and hear a few more battle stations incinerate. I turn my face away from the screen so I can open my eyes and look at the aquarium—

still not looking at the game.

The tetras are swimming nervously toward the water's surface, the clown loaches are bouncing around the center, and the angelfish are in a slow orbit around Victor. The catfish, as usual, is poking around in the gravel. I see myself floating above a reef in Bermuda, fish all around me, sometimes brushing up against me. I dive down to get a better look at an anemone or sea star. Then I swim out to a shipwreck and dive under to check out the great, gray, rusting hulk, home to colonies of barnacles. Any treasure that was ever here has been recovered by divers before me. What about the passengers on the ship? Did they drown in a storm? Or did they swim away safely to shore? How did they get wrecked anyway, so close to the island? They probably thought they were perfectly safe when—BAM!—the ship's hull caught on a huge rock or reef, invisible from the surface. But when you see it from underwater, you wonder how anybody could miss it.

"Hey, Gabe, whatcha doing?" It's Maxie. "I think you're about to get really, really blown up."

"Whee-yuh! Whee-yuh!"

"Stop it, Maxie!" I yell.

"It's not me," he says.

I turn back to the computer screen. While I was off diving in Bermuda, the Zygurts built a bunch of battle stations

94

and my Stealth Satellites got bumped out of orbit, and now the Zygurts are bombarding London and Tokyo with exploding drones. And we know what that sounds like.

"Whee-yuh! Whee-yuh!"

"This stupid game!" I exclaim.

"Let me take over, Gabe! Please! Let me fight the drones!" Maxie reaches for the joystick.

I sit and watch. Maxie quickly sends up some new Stealth Satellites and launches a barrage of missiles, some of which actually destroy a few Zygurt battle stations. But I gave the Zygurts an awfully good head start. Now the drones are speeding toward Buenos Aires, Moscow, and Beijing.

"Whee-yuh! Whee-yuh!"

"Oh, be quiet!" Maxie yells. "You stupid Whee-yuhs!" And then he reaches up to the sound dial and turns the volume off. No more Whee-yuhs.

Maxie holds off Earth's total annihilation for a good five minutes. But when I went off on my imaginary dive, I basically delivered Earth to the invaders from Beyond. Maxie can only delay humanity's sad fate for so long.

The earth disappears in a final firestorm. Maxie hands the joystick back to me. "Well, we tried," he says.

"Maxie, breakfast," Mom calls from the kitchen, and then he's gone.

I switch to *DeepSea*. I have a few minutes left before we

leave for school, so I click until I get to the saved game where Victor and I are searching for the wreck of the *Victoriana.* We swim safely into uncharted waters. That's one of the things you want to do in the game, because then when you get back to the laboratory, the computer maps out the new territory for you and that helps the next time you're looking for the shipwreck. But if you die in uncharted waters, you don't get to claim it as explored new territory, and it doesn't get mapped back at the laboratory.

We dodge some poisonous stingrays, pet a harmless manta ray, and avoid a strong current that carries away the rays, a shark we hadn't seen, and a school of mackerel. My attention is captured by some spiny lionfish swimming above us. You don't see them very often, and they are totally cool, even though they're poisonous. I saw them in real life once at the National Aquarium in Baltimore. I swim over for a closer look at their mane-like spikes and puffed-up bodies. I circle around and swim along with them, pointing my underwater camera in the hope of framing a good picture. You get extra points for bringing photographs back to the lab.

Just when I see that I've got a nice picture—disaster strikes. I'm attacked from below. I mean, I'm really clobbered. It's a gray shark, and I don't have a chance. I never even saw it.

But Victor had stayed down deeper when I went up to

look at the lionfish. He must have seen the shark down there. Normally he would say, in his tinny computer voice, "Shark alert! Remember, Gabe, stay very still." Why did my diving buddy let me down?

It's time to go to school. I exit out of the game, then click on the shut-down command that appears on the screen. I wait for the chime that rings when the computer is turning off. "Dee-doo-dee," it always sounds. I wait, but the computer is quiet, and then it is off.

Now I remember. Maxie had turned the sound off so we didn't have to listen to the "whee-yuh!" noises of the Zygurt drones. Victor probably had warned me. But I couldn't hear him.

Chapter Eleven

See It on the Big Screen

I have a conflict-free day at school, but not because I'm thinking of Dad's suggestions. It's just that nobody makes any insulting remarks. Nothing happens that bothers me. In science, it's my turn to record the observations of Ecosystem Number 5. We had to start all over again after Derek and I dumped our eco-column on the floor, so there's not much of interest to report. Derek, Zach, Elise, and I all agree that there are no visible changes since last week. In our notebook I faithfully record our discussion of this non-event, which is either that not enough time has passed for the guppies to have babies or the moss to spread—or that our ecosystem is already dying.

"Want to come over after school?" I ask Evan on the

walk home. Maxie is skipping ahead of us.

"Sure," Evan says.

"I feel like making set-ups with action figures," I say, knowing that Evan is always game to do that.

"Me, too," Evan says. "I'll be over in a few minutes." We say good-bye at his house.

Mom's home, as usual. She checks in with Jake, makes sure Maxie eats something before he runs outside where he hopes to be able to play in the street soccer game again, and urges me to go outdoors.

"Evan's coming over," I say. "We're going to play with figures. Maybe we'll go out after."

Then Mom runs upstairs to make her calls, and Evan is at the door. He's carrying a grocery bag full of stuff—figures and scenery and props for space set-ups, underwater scenes, knights and castles, and modern-day soldiers. We spread out his stuff with mine in the computer room.

Evan and I make a great combination underwater-and-space universe and take turns playing the good guys and the bad guys. The bad guys want to invade and take over WaterSpace, a space/sea galaxy, otherwise known as my aquarium. The good guys have to repulse this attack on WaterSpace because the invasion will mean certain death for the beautiful and peaceful citizens of that galaxy, who cannot survive if alien beings invade their environment.

The good guys also want to help save WaterSpace because if it is destroyed, its waters will flood the rest of the universe—meaning certain death for us all. Not that the bad guys care. They, and only they, have special space/sea suits and gear that will protect them.

Of course, we don't actually touch the aquarium because we don't want to upset the fish. But we have a great time.

"You know what would be so cool?" I say when we've finished our fifth battle. Bad guys lie lifeless all over the floor. The fish swim safely in their WaterSpace.

"What?" Evan says.

"If we made our own movie. Film the story of the defense of WaterSpace. *WaterSpace: The Movie*."

"You've seen it on stage," Evan announces dramatically. "You've seen the heroes in the toy store. Now see the story as you've never seen it before: on the big screen. The epic saga of the attack on the peace-loving galaxy of WaterSpace. The unbelievable bravery of those who defend the galaxy. The action, the beauty, the mystery—coming soon to a theater near you."

"You know, if we had a video camera, we really could do it," I say.

"Jeez, doesn't your Dad have every type of electronic device known to mankind?" Evan asks. "I thought he gets all that stuff from his store."

"He doesn't work in a store," I say. "It's an office."

"Oh, right," Evan says. "He's an office supply salesman."

"He's not a salesman in a store anyone can just walk into," I say.

I don't know why I'm suddenly feeling so touchy. But now that I've started, I want to make sure Evan understands. "My dad sells stuff to big businesses and to the government. The computers and office machines they sell are kept in warehouses. Dad has an office and when he needs to, he goes to his customers. They don't come to a store."

"Okay, whatever," Evan says. "So, as I was saying, I thought he gets all that electronic stuff from his *office*. He still sells the stuff out of his *office*, right?"

Is Evan putting down my dad because he's a salesman? Evan's mom and dad are both lawyers. But that's not what Evan said, or even suggested, is it? I shake my head quickly like I'm trying to clear it of static. The static is Evan's tone when he talks about my dad's job. It's my annoyance at having to explain that Dad doesn't work in a store. It's aggravation because our video camera broke and is beyond repair.

"Anyway, it doesn't matter," Evan continues. "We have a video camera. I'll get it. Be right back."

I close my eyes and try to float above the static. But

that's where the noise is, where the waves chop-chop-chop at me. So I dive instead, head down to where it's quiet and dark and I can get away from the turbulence. By the time Evan returns, I'm actually calm. Maybe this stuff works.

Evan plugs the camera into the wall outlet, and we start shooting a scene. The camera focuses automatically, so we don't have to worry about that. Instead, we can concentrate on zooming in for close-ups and zooming out for wide-angle views. Evan doesn't have a tripod, so we rest the camera on the kitchen stepstool when we want it to be very steady.

Evan tells me about a magazine article he read about "stop-action" videography. It's a way to make figures and other objects appear to move by themselves in a video. First you set up the scene. You put a good guy crawling on his belly on the floor, say. The idea is that he's sneaking up on the bad guys. They're a few feet away, huddled together planning a battle. You press the "record" button on the camera, just long enough to film the scene for a few seconds. You keep the camera in exactly the same position—in our case, on the kitchen stepstool—and you move the characters ever so slightly. So the guy on his belly advances a centimeter or two, the guys in the huddle maybe shift their feet or arms. Then you film again for a few seconds. You move the belly guy and the huddle guys again, just slightly. Film for a few seconds. And on and on, until the scene is done—the good guy ambushes the bad guys, or whatever.

What a pain! Nobody ever said making movies was easy. But it's basically the same thing as making a flipbook, only instead of stapling the pictures together in a book and flipping them to see the drawings move, you push a button and—*ta-dah!*—you have a movie.

This is just the greatest. I can't believe we've never thought to do this before. You need lots of patience to film a scene this way. But it's worth the effort. The camera has playback, so we can review what we've just filmed. Our first attempts are kind of rough and shaky, but we improve as we practice.

"Okay," I say after we've taped about twenty seconds of a scene that takes place on the floor, "now let's try a space scene." While we were taping the first scene, I'd been thinking about how to film guys moving through the air. It's a challenge. You don't want to move them around with your hands like you do when you're playing, because then you'd have your hands in the movie. I'm thinking we might use string, very thin string—thread. Tie the thread on the guys or spaceships or whatever and move them around. I explain my idea to Evan and run into the kitchen where Mom keeps the sewing stuff in a box in one of the drawers.

"I have white thread and light blue thread," I say. "We'll see which one blends into the background better."

We tie both kinds of thread onto a spaceship and onto a guy who is outfitted with a jet-propelling device on his back. I'm the cameraman for this take; Evan is in charge of moving the actors and making sounds.

"B-b-r-r-r-w-w-w." He blows air through his flapping lips, making a sound that's supposed to be a motor. At the same time he lifts the suspended spaceship and space guy an inch or so off the ground. I record the action. I think he's moved them too fast.

"Hold them where they are!" I call out after I stop recording. "Next time, move them slower and smoother. One, two, three, action!" I push the record button again. Evan repeats his noises and actions.

"Stop!" I yell and stop recording. "Don't move them so much, okay? Ready? One, two, three, action!" I push the record button. Evan does his thing. This time it looks like he moves the figures two inches higher.

"If you keep doing it that way, it'll look all jerky in the movie," I complain. "Remember how slowly we moved the stuff on the floor?"

"Hey, you try holding these things in mid-air for a while," Evan says. "My arms are starting to hurt. Anyway, we should look at playback to see whether your thread idea works."

"I don't think we'll be able to tell yet," I say. "A few more shots."

"No, man, I want to know if it's worth it," Evan says. "My muscles are twitching."

"We won't be able to tell yet," I repeat. "Come on, don't be a wimp."

"Don't be a jerk," Evan says. "You're bossing me around like you think you're Steven Spielberg or something."

"Can I help it if I want to do this right?" I say. "Listen. Three more shots is all I ask."

While we've been talking, Evan has relaxed his arms to rest the spaceship and space guy on the floor. "Oh, all right," he says.

But he doesn't end up in the same position he was in when we were first filming. Plus, for each of the three filming takes, he lifts the figures up too fast and too high.

"That's it," he says after the third take. He lets the toys clatter to the floor. "All that work, and we don't even know whether it looks right."

"Well, we'll see right now," I say.

We look at the playback. The movement is just like I thought—very jerky and unnatural-looking. Also, for the last three takes Evan forgot to make the motor noises so all you can hear on the tape is me breathing.

I look at Evan. Before I can say anything, he says, "You can see the strings. You can see the white ones and the blue ones. I knew it wouldn't work. What did you think? They'd magically become invisible?"

"I didn't hear you suggest a better idea," I say.

"I didn't have a chance. You rushed us into this. I think we should spread a blue blanket on the floor and put it over a chair and use it as a space background. Then we could move the figures and stuff around normally, without all these stupid threads, and it would look like it was happening in space because of the background. Instead we wasted forty-five minutes on a dumb puppet show."

"No," I say, "it wasn't a dumb puppet show. The problem isn't that you can see the threads a tiny bit—it's that the action was all jerky. And we know whose fault that is."

"The only jerky thing around here is you!" Evan says. "Give me my camera! I'm outta here." He puts everything in his box and heads for the front door

"Yeah, I don't know why I thought we could do a movie together," I yell after him. "You'll never have any good ideas."

"And you'll never have any friends," he hisses.

Then the door slams.

Chapter Twelve

Thomas Gets His Tank

"Have we forgotten anything?" Dominique asks. I'm about to answer him but see by the slight frown on this forehead that he's really talking to himself. He looks through the three boxes of aquarium equipment that he's carefully assembled. "Okay," he says. "We're all set."

It's Tuesday, and Dominique, Thomas Doherty, and I are walking the three boxes over to Thomas's apartment to set up his new aquarium.

"Here we are," Thomas says. "Here we are." His apartment is on the ground floor of the three-story brick building. Thomas's front door is blue with a brass "2" above the doorbell.

Thomas jiggles his keys and opens the door. "Come in," he says. He's humming a tune I don't recognize. "This is my home, sweet home."

The apartment is basically one large room. Against one

wall is a bed with a cover and cushions on it, making it look like a sofa. There's also a chair with a footstool, a television on a stand, and a bookcase stacked mostly with kids' books. The other side of the room has a small stove with only two burners, a narrow oven, a refrigerator about half the size of the one we have at home, and a little table with two chairs.

"You have a nice place, Thomas," Dominique says. "Good light, too." He strolls to the window. "Look, you can see our shopping center."

"But you can't see the fish store," Thomas says.

"No," Dominique agrees, "only the drugstore." He notices a small, empty table near the television. "Is this for the aquarium, Thomas?"

"Yup," Thomas says. "My sister gave me that table. It was extra in her house."

"O-kay," Dominique flashes his white teeth. "Let's do it."

We unpack the boxes on the floor in front of the little table. "Can I help you?" Thomas asks.

"Well, first we need to wash the tank and the gravel," Dominique says.

"I have this dishwashing soap," Thomas says. "It smells real nice." He walks to the kitchen sink to get the bottle of detergent.

"We only need water," says Dominique. "Soap is poisonous to fish. Let's just wash out the tank in your kitchen sink." He takes the stuff to the kitchen and looks in the cabinet under the sink. "Have you got a bucket? You can wash out the gravel in a bucket."

Thomas doesn't have a bucket in his apartment, but he knows where one is in the building's laundry room. He also knows where the outside hose is hooked up. Dominique tells him to make sure he washes out the bucket first, and only then he should pour in the gravel and hose it down.

"You can do that, can't you, Thomas?" Dominique asks.

"Sure, I can do that, Dom-Dom," Thomas says. "I'll be back with clean gravel soon." He takes the bag of blue gravel he picked out at the store and heads out the door.

I wait for Dominique to follow Thomas. I assume he's going to supervise, but instead Dominique wrestles the tank into the small kitchen sink and begins to rinse it carefully.

"Should I go—?" I gesture toward the door.

"With Thomas?" Dominique finishes for me. "If you want. But I could use your help here getting things ready for the tank."

I have visions of Thomas dumping blue gravel all over the grass and then trying to pick up each stone, one by one, and dropping them back into the bucket. You wouldn't want little pieces of grass and dirt in a new aquarium. But Dominique seems unconcerned, so I find the filter, air pump, thermometer, and plastic ferns and get them ready to be placed into the aquarium.

"So, school ends next week, hey, Gabe?" Dominique says. The tank is clean. He's drying it. "What are you doing with your summer?"

My plans for the summer: This is a major topic of conversation at our house. I don't have plans for the summer, and that's a problem. Not a problem for me, but for Mom and Dad. If I'm not in a camp or school or something, who is going to keep an eye on me? Until I'm thirteen, my parents want me to have some kind of supervision. Maxie is going to a day camp where they do sports and arts-and-crafts and outdoor stuff. He loves all that junk. Jake is enrolled in a special program for talented kids at a local art school. Mom and Dad tried to get me to sign up for some kind of day camp but, as I see it, going to camp means trying to get along with a new group of kids that I really don't want to hang out with anyway.

One thing I have been planning to do is to join the swim team at our neighborhood pool. I'm a decent swimmer. But there's a problem: This plan kind of depends on Evan and me being friends. We were going to do it together, and his housekeeper, Martha, was going to drive us to the swim practices and pick us up. Evan's mom even said I could hang around at their house whenever I wanted. Mom and Dad weren't thrilled about that. They told me they didn't feel they should take advantage of the fact that Evan has a full-time housekeeper who wasn't being paid to look after me. But they also didn't say no.

Now, though, I'm in a major bind. If Evan and I aren't friends anymore, I can't exactly plan my summer around him. I find myself telling Dominique about our fight over the stop-action movie.

"I guess I was kind of tough on him," I tell Dominique. "But I wanted to do it right. I mean, I'd never made a movie before. Suddenly I had this great camera to work with, and so many ideas . . ."

I trail off. I don't want to tell Dominique about how hard it is for me to get along with other kids, especially since I like hanging out with him.

"It's hard to be sensitive to other people when you're totally into something," Dominique says. "All you want to do is this thing you're excited about. You don't want anyone interfering with it—messing it up."

"Yeah," I say. "If I made a movie by myself, it would probably turn out better."

"Maybe so," Dominique says. "So why don't you?"

"Make my own movie, you mean?"

Dominique nods.

"Well, for one thing, I don't have a working video camera at the moment."

"That's the reason?"

"Yeah, if I had my own camera, I'd make my own stop-action videos. I'd be the director, producer, scriptwriter, everything."

"So pretend today's your lucky day," Dominique says. "Imagine you're doing all that with your own camera, all by yourself. Is it what you want to be doing?"

"Didn't I just say so?"

"Yes, you just said so, but you're allowed to say things and still be thinking about them."

I think for a minute. "Okay," I say. "The good thing is it would be a better movie if I did it by myself. The bad thing is, there'd be no one else to bounce ideas off of, and no one else to see it coming together. With Evan, the movie wasn't going to be as good as it could have been, but until we started fighting, it was fun."

"So making the movie was fun, even though the movie wasn't going to win any Academy Awards."

I snicker. "Or even any Kids' Choice Awards on Nickelodeon."

"So what do you think now?" Dominique asks.

"I guess I have to choose between wanting to win Academy Awards and wanting to have friends."

"Do you?" Dominique asks. "Do you have to choose between Academy Awards and friends?"

"Looks that way."

"Oh."

I hear the disagreement in Dominique's voice, so I add, "Look, that's what it always seems to come down to. I can try to keep my ideas and feelings under the surface so that I don't act up and kids will want to hang out with me. Or I can be myself, the guy who wants things to be right—"

"You mean 'right' according to you?"

"—yeah, whatever, and I'll be mean to other kids, and they'll all make fun of me and hate me."

"There's nothing in between?" Dominique interrupts.

Just then Thomas is back with a bucket of gravel. "All clean," he announces.

Dominique looks inside the bucket and nods. "Let's spread it in the tank," he says.

The three of us—mainly Dominique and me, with Thomas humming—assemble the aquarium. We add water slowly, one glassful at a time, to avoid stirring up the gravel. I try anchoring the artificial plants under the gravel, but they keep floating up.

"Aw, you do it," I say to Dominique.

"Keep trying," he says, so I do and manage to get the plants secured on the bottom. Then we add more glassfuls of water—this is a job for Thomas—and put in special water treatment drops to neutralize any dangerous chemicals or minerals in the tap water. Next come the filter, water pump, heater, and thermometer. Finally, we plug everything into the electrical outlet underneath the table where the aquarium sits. Once we do that, water begins to bubble through the air pump and filter, and the little heater clicks on. Dominique sets the heater to seventy-four degrees Fahrenheit. He shows Thomas how to read the thermometer and tells him to check it later to make sure the water temperature is not below seventy-two degrees or above seventy-six degrees.

"When do we get fish?" Thomas asks.

"Thursday or Friday," Dominique says. Thomas blinks his eyes, but doesn't say anything.

I sit back on my heels and look at the tank. I notice that the gravel is unevenly spread. Also, I clumped the plants together a little too much on the left side of the aquarium, leaving the right half of the tank looking kind of bare. I also put in a little ceramic figure—a diver, but not the same as my Victor—and now I see that he would look better if I had faced him more toward the front of the tank.

"Good work, team," Dominique says.

"It looks beautiful," Thomas says. "Thanks, Dom-Dom. Thank you, Gabe."

I decide not to point out the flaws.

"We work well together, Gabe," Dominique says. "Do you think your parents would let you add a part-time job at Tanks for You to your busy summer schedule?"

Chapter Thirteen

Sucked into the DeepSea Canyon

Once again, I'm submerged, deep underwater, far from sunshine, waves, and gulls. Only this time, I'm far from coral reefs and beautiful fish and shipwrecks and treasure. I'm playing *DeepSea Canyon*, DeepDown Software's long-awaited new game and it is—not perfect. Very cool, but not perfect.

When you play, you're a deep-sea explorer, and the object is to make it to Earth's core, which I haven't done, and Dominique hasn't either. You wander down through levels of weird and fantastic life, plants, and sometimes other hostile divers who are also trying to get to the core. As you descend, you must make adjustments to your equipment, using a pull-down menu of options that is just a little bit too complicated for me. But I guess my way through it.

You have to keep a steady hand and head as you dive because you want to avoid extremes of temperature and pressure and avoid the underwater currents that might pull you down or up too suddenly. The main goal is to reach the core, but you get points for avoiding, rather than destroying, poisonous sea life as you descend. After all, you're on a peaceful mission to the center of the earth, where scientists believe we may find elements that will fight disease on the surface. Also, some poisonous creatures contain venoms and other things that may be useful to humans, so you get points for successfully trapping and sending them up to the surface. For every one hundred points, you're rewarded with a film clip of real underwater sea life of a coral reef—cool-looking creatures like sea anemones, rays, sharks, marlins, and octopuses.

The clock in the bottom right-hand corner of the computer screen tells me it's 8:28 AM.

"My bus is here," I hear Maxie call, followed by my mother's footsteps running down the stairs. She must have been in her bedroom getting ready to go to the office.

"Bye, little guy," she says, and I can tell by Maxie's muffled "bye" that she's pulled him against her for a hug. Then comes the slam of the screen door, Mom calling, "Have fun!" and the grinding of the camp bus as it carries Maxie off to his day.

"Five minutes, Jake!" Mom calls to my other brother

who's in the kitchen eating breakfast. He doesn't answer.

"Jake, do you hear?" Mom says, hesitating on the steps.

"I hear," he says. "I'm just eating and trying to find something. . . ." His voice becomes impossible to hear. I pause my game to get up and peer around the corner into the kitchen. As I suspected, he's munching a toaster pastry and digging through his junk drawer. Since starting the summer art class three weeks ago, Jake's collection of stuff has grown like crazy. Mom had to give him a bigger drawer to hold all the junk he's been finding.

"Are you sure you really need all these things you're bringing into the house?" she asked last week before she offered him the new drawer. "I don't want to fill my kitchen with a bunch of garbage."

Jake looked hurt. "Does this look like garbage?" he asked, holding up a penny that had been mangled under some great weight, maybe a train wheel. "Does this? Or this? How about this?" He displayed a short length of spiral telephone cord, an envelope with four colorful Malaysian stamps on it, and a section of bicycle chain.

Jake got his expanded storage space. Every few days he rummages through it for something he wants to use in an art project at summer school. He seems to enjoy his class as much as Maxie loves his camp.

As for me, the summer has turned out okay so far.

Every weekday morning Mom and Jake leave together. She drops him off at art school and then heads to her office. I'm by myself for about fifteen minutes. Then I walk over to Evan's and we go to the morning swim practice together. It runs from 9:00 to 11:00. Martha comes to the pool when practice is over, and we either stay there until lunch or, if we're wiped out, go back to Evan's house. I usually eat with Evan and Martha, and then I'm off to Tanks for You for my part-time job.

My job is *at* the store, but not exactly *with* the store. I'm actually working for this organization—Potomac Area Aquarium Society—whose members are aquarium hobbyists and tropical fish fanatics from around our community. Mr. Newman is president of the group, and he needed someone to organize their computer stuff over the summer. The membership list is half-computerized and half-scribbled in a spiral notebook. The Web site hasn't been updated for six months. I may be forty years younger than Mr. Newman, but I've got way more experience with computers.

Once I'm done organizing the membership list, I've got big plans for the Web site. Anything would be an improvement. I mean, here's a site about fantastic-looking fish, and right now it's got no photos at all, just a few lame-looking clipart pictures. And members should be able to post messages about all kinds of aquarium topics. This is basic stuff, but the PAAS's Web site doesn't have any of it yet.

When Dominique first suggested me for the job, Mr. Newman seemed a little doubtful that a twelve-and-a-half-year-old could handle it. But when I showed him how easy all the computer stuff was for me, he was cool with it. It's a volunteer job, not a paid one, but I don't really care. I get to go to Tanks for You (because that's where Mr. Newman keeps all the papers for the society), work on the computer there, and hang out with Dominique and the fish. And Mr. Newman lets me buy my aquarium supplies for half off. I think it's a sweet deal.

Most days, I work two or three hours, until around 3:30. Then I walk home, where I meet Mom and Jake, who have usually just gotten back from Jake's art school. Then Maxie's bus pulls up in front of the house, and he tumbles out, full of news about his day.

So things have worked out pretty well. Of course, one reason it all came together was that I made up with Evan after our big fight over our movie. We both said we were sorry and agreed that we kind of lost it that day because we kept working on the movie longer than we should have. We've worked with the camera since then and tried out his idea for stop-action scenes that take place in space—using a blue blanket as a space backdrop and moving figures around in front of it. No threads attached to anything, no hanging anything in the air. The final movie looked like a bunch of action figures moving around a blue blanket, but I didn't say that. I don't think Evan was very happy with it either. Now we've turned our attention to live-action movies—filming real people and real things.

Maxie says we should make a movie of him in a musical. He'll make it all up, he says, the story, the songs, the dancing. Fortunately, Maxie's at camp when Evan and I are together, and when he comes home from camp, he's so tired he doesn't have enough energy to bother me about it. That's a good thing, because his idea doesn't have a chance. Evan and I plan to make a documentary—to film a story in real life. We haven't chosen our topic yet, so we film a lot of things just for practice.

"Be careful, Gabe," Mom says to me this morning as she leans over to kiss me goodbye. I'm back at the computer.

"You're afraid I'm going to be sucked down the DeepSea Canyon?" I ask. "I didn't know you cared."

"Ha," she says. "See you this afternoon."

Mom's been telling me to be careful every morning for the past three weeks, since summer began. I don't have to ask what she wants me to be careful about anymore. Be careful not to let strangers in the house during the fifteen minutes I'm by myself, be careful to lock up when I leave, be careful not to drown at swim practice, be careful not to get run over by a car during my walk to the shopping center. A few careful minutes later, I'm at the pool doing my first set of laps with the team. I like the way my body and all its parts and muscles move and feel in the water. In the water, my legs and feet, which feel heavy and clumsy on the soccer field, are transformed into propellers and a rudder, all working together, powerfully and efficiently. Not that I'm the best swimmer on the team—not even close. But I'm also not even close to being the worst, and I can feel my own strength and energy when I swim, which is such a great feeling. I don't even mind the chill of the water at our early-morning practices or the sting of the chlorine in my eyes.

The breaststroke is my best stroke. This year I'm about the best breaststroker in my age group, eleven- and twelve-year-old boys. Compared with the other strokes—freestyle, butterfly, and backstroke—I guess it is the slowest way to get from one end of the pool to the other, but breaststroke seems to suit me. Maybe it's the long underwater beginning and the fact that the stroke and kick take place underwater. It's the closest stroke there is to underwater diving. I find it almost relaxing to swim breaststroke, even in a swim meet when all the kids are yelling and cheering. I just concentrate on my arm pulls and my glides and my frog kick, and I don't even know the other kids are there. I haven't lost a breaststroke race in any of the swim meets our team has had this season.

"Hey, Gabe," a voice calls. I'm stretched out on the deck recovering from swimming twenty laps non-stop, the last leg of our workout. My eyes are closed.

It doesn't sound like Evan, and I'd be surprised if Evan was finished yet. He usually gets worn out after ten laps, and the rest is very slow going.

I open my eyes. It's Zach, the Zach who was in my class and in my ecosystem group, Derek's sidekick, only Derek doesn't come to this pool so Zach is kind of on his own at swim-team events.

"Hi, Zach," I say.

"Want to practice turns with me after you've taken your breather?" he asks.

"I'm not taking a breather, Zach," I say. "I'm done with practice. I'm just waiting for Evan."

"I'm done, too," he says. "So—do you want to practice flip turns while you're waiting?"

I have zero interest in getting back in the water. He'd probably think I'm a wimp if I tell him I feel chilly and tired, so I say, "Nah—you know, I do an open turn for breaststroke."

In competition, we swim fifty meters—two lengths of the pool. When you swim freestyle or backstroke, you usually do a flip turn—like an underwater somersault—when you reach the end of the first twenty-five meters. For breaststroke and butterfly, where you have to touch the wall with two hands, some people flip on the turn, and some don't. I don't. Instead, I double-touch as quickly as I can, twist my body around, and push off. That's an open turn.

Zach considers what I've said and nods. "Oh, right. Hey, your breaststroke is *great* this summer, Gabe. Really great."

Am I being set up for some kind of put-down? I can already hear it coming out of Zach's mouth: "Really great for a *girl's* stroke, Gabe." "Hey, your *breast* is really developing, Gabe. Soon you'll need a bra, right?"

I wait, but no insult comes. "Well, thanks, Zach," I say. "Your backstroke looks good, too." I can tell Zach is proud of his stroke.

"Thanks," he says. "I swam over the winter. It really helped. When I started the season this summer, my time was already a whole second better than my best time last summer. You should winter-swim next year, Gabe."

"Well, maybe I will," I say. After all, it's not like I would have to juggle winter swimming with all my *other* sports activities.

As if he's reading my mind, Zach adds, "Since you don't do soccer or basketball or anything."

Okay, I'm ready. Now comes the put-down.

But Zach just grins and says, "I drove my mom nuts last winter, running around to a million different practices. I drove myself nuts, too. Next winter, I'm going to cut some things out. You know, a guy can't do it all."

Just then, Evan flops down beside me. He's breathing so hard, I'm a little worried he's going to pass out or something. But I'm only a little worried. This is how Evan gets at the end of his twenty laps. He'll be okay in a few minutes.

"So, are you guys hanging out at the pool now?" Zach asks.

I look at the clock. It's 11:15. Practice was officially over at 11:00, except for kids who were still swimming their twenty.

"We're going to have lunch at my house," Evan says, still panting. "Then Gabe has to go to work, and I have a clarinet lesson."

"You have a *job*?" Zach says to me.

I explain about the Potomac Area Aquarium Society as I shake the last few drops of water from my ear.

"Cool," Zach says. "How much do you get paid?"

I tell him it's a volunteer job.

"Rip-off," Zach says.

"Not really," I say. "It's fun. No one gets paid for doing PAAS work."

"Anyway," Evan cuts in, "kids our age can't have paying jobs, other than something like baby-sitting or cutting grass. It's the law."

Evan would know something like that, with his two lawyer parents.

"Well," Zach says. "I hate cutting grass and wouldn't baby-sit for a million dollars. So I guess I'd rather have your job. How'd you get it?"

Do I remind him that I have my own aquarium? Do I say that he could have ended up with the job if he'd stuck with his goldfish bowl when he was a little kid?

Forget it. I'm in a hurry, and Zach may not remember the fight I had with Derek when the two of them teased me about my aquarium. All I say is, "Oh, you know how these things go. The job just sort of happened."

"Martha's here," Evan announces.

"Maybe I'll stop by to see you at work one of these days," says Zach.

"Okay," I say. Evan and I hurry toward the parking lot.

"He's an idiot," Evan says on the drive home.

I don't answer. Zach seemed smaller somehow, away from school, away from Derek. Of course, he has probably actually grown bigger since the end of school. He just didn't seem to be as annoying and insulting as he used to be.

Back at Evan's house, I change into dry clothes and wolf down two peanut butter sandwiches.

"What're you doing until your clarinet lesson?" I ask Evan.

"I think I'll fool around with the video camera," he says. "And play computer games."

Evan also has the new *DeepSea* game. We quickly compare notes on our progress toward the earth's core.

"Try adjusting the diver's mouthpiece controls after you're down to two hundred and fifty feet," I say. "Otherwise, the air supply gets funny." I learned that the hard way the other day.

I walk the six blocks to the store, where Dominique is busy with a new customer. Dominique is good with newbies. He takes the time to explain what's involved in setting up and caring for an aquarium. He helps people figure out what to buy. And almost every time, even though he mentions at the very beginning that the tank has to be up and running for a couple of days before fish can live in it, the newbies look like someone stole their candy when they go to pick out their new pets and Dominique reminds them that it's too early. We always share a smile over that.

"I think I'd like an angelfish, two of those black-and-orange ones, and some of the little silvery ones." The newbie is a woman who has selected a smallish tank, just twenty gallons.

"Well, you can have them if you want to kill them," Dominique tells her point-blank.

Whoa! That's not Dominique *at all.* I look for a big

grin to signal that he's joking, but no. I try to catch his eye, but he's looking down at the pad where he's adding up the woman's purchases.

"Oh," she says. She looks shocked. "Well, of course, I wouldn't want to do that."

Dominique just shakes his head, still bent over the receipt.

"I don't understand," the woman says.

This is so strange. I normally don't talk very much to customers, but this is not a normal situation, so I say, "He just means the tank won't be ready for the fish for a few days. You're supposed to wait until the water is ready before you add the fish."

Now Dominique looks up. "Yeah, I think that was the first thing I told you. Remember?"

The woman pays quickly. When I ask whether she would like help getting the stuff to her car, she says no.

The store seems awfully quiet after that. I sit in front of the computer and check for messages in the PAAS e-mail box. I want to ask Dominique what's up, but I can tell there's a wall around him—and I'm sort of afraid to try to get through.

The door opens again, and Thomas Doherty walks in. Once inside, he keeps walking. He walks up and down the three aisles in the middle of the store. He walks around the outside aisle past the display tanks set up against the walls. As he walks, he blinks quickly and clicks his tongue against his teeth. After he's made one trip around the entire store, up and down all the aisles, he makes another. And another. And then another, never stopping to look at anything, not even the new purple angelfish.

Normally Dominique would say something like, "Hi, Thomas, how's it going?" or "What's your water temperature?" which he knows Thomas checks every day, twice a day. But today Dominique says nothing. He stands silently behind the cash register, busy with some paperwork. I've never seen him so busy with paperwork.

Finally, Thomas stops clicking long enough to speak. "My fish are very calm. Very, very calm."

This causes Dominique to look up. I stop reading e-mail.

"Very, very, very calm," Thomas repeats.

Chapter Fourteen

The Constant Hum

Fortunately, Mr. Newman shows up soon after Thomas to give Dominique a lunch break. Dominique, Thomas, and I rush over to Thomas's apartment.

Thomas is right, in a way. These fish are calm as calm can be. They're floating on their sides like tiny, colorful pancakes. Dead. Every single one.

Dominique scoops the lifeless fish out with a little paper cup and flushes them down the toilet. He says nothing except, finally, when he leans into the tank to make sure he's gotten all the fish and he takes a whiff.

"It smells like laundry soap," he says. "How come the aquarium water smells like detergent?"

"I put some in," mumbles Thomas.

"You put *laundry detergent* in the fish tank?" says Dominique. I've never heard his voice take on a tone like that. "That's what happened? You put *laundry soap* in here?"

Thomas nods miserably.

"It's poisonous to fish, Thomas," Dominique says. "I told you soap was poisonous to the fish the day we set this aquarium up. The detergent killed them!"

Thomas is still nodding, but somehow his words and his head have gotten out of synch, because what he says is, "No, no. No, no, Dom-Dom. Not the detergent."

"Yes, yes. Yes, yes, Tom-Tom. You killed your fish with detergent."

Now Thomas switches from nodding to shaking his head. "It was my sister. She doesn't want to do my laundry at her house anymore. She says to use the washing machines in my building. But I don't like the laundry room here. It has spiders. I saw them in there that day we made my aquarium. When I got the bucket from the laundry room. I don't want to do my laundry here, I told my sister—"

"Listen, Thomas," Dominique interrupts him, which causes Thomas immediately to start clicking. "I have to get back to the store. You empty out the water from the tank, and then wash the stuff inside. I can't do it for you now." Dominique turns to go.

"Should I—should I come with you or help Thomas?" I ask.

"I can't stay," Dominique says. "Mr. Newman isn't paying me to clean out Thomas's tank."

"Oh—but I need help!" Thomas says. "I could make a big mess or break something or—"

Dominique interrupts him again, this time to talk to me. "You want to help Thomas, Gabe?"

I nod. "I don't mind."

"Fine." And then he leaves.

I turn to Thomas. "Okay," I say. "I guess we need to empty out the water first. One cup at a time."

Thomas gets two plastic drinking cups from his kitchen cabinet. We need the bucket, but I'm worried about asking Thomas for it because of what he's just said about the spiders in the laundry room. So I say, "If you tell me where the laundry room is, Thomas, I'll go get the bucket so we can dump the water in it."

Instead, Thomas goes to the little closet by the door of his apartment and takes out a new-looking red plastic bucket. "I bought one," he says.

When I crouch down to unplug the aquarium's electrical cords before we start to bail out the water, I find that they're already unplugged. I'm pretty sure Dominique didn't unplug them. You have to sort of crawl down under the table to reach the electrical outlet, and I didn't see Dominique do that. But I'm also surprised that Thomas would think to unplug the cords—even though a tank of dead fish doesn't need a working air pump, filter, and heater.

"Were you saving on your electric bill?" I ask Thomas, holding up the cords. I sort of mean it as a joke.

"No," Thomas says, and he looks so sad, but he stops clicking. "No," he says again, and he starts shaking his head like he did before, and I can tell he wants to talk, wants to tell the story that Dominique cut off, about his sister and the laundry and the fish.

"No?" I say.

"I told my sister I don't like the laundry room. It's dark and scary. It's got spiders. But she says I'll get used to the laundry room. And she says she'll come over here, and we can do my laundry together. She hasn't been to my apartment for a long time. She helped me clean it when I moved in. I wanted to make it clean for her."

So you put laundry detergent in the fish tank? I almost interrupt, but keep my mouth shut.

"I cleaned my furniture and my windows, and I used the vacuum cleaner on the floor. I wanted to clean my whole apartment, and the only place to plug in the vacuum cleaner is here." Thomas points to the electrical outlet behind the aquarium table. "I had to unplug the tank's cords so I could put in this big vacuum cleaner plug. And I forgot—"

He forgot. He forgot to plug the aquarium back into the socket, and a day and a half later his pretty purple angelfish, lemon tetras, and catfish were floating on their sides in the middle of the tank, dead.

"I shouldn't have forgotten," Thomas says, hitting the side of his head with his hand. "And next day it smelled bad . . ." Thomas must have put in a capful of detergent to keep the tank from getting too smelly.

I'm not sure what to say. What's the right thing to say to a man who's just come out of his closed-off little world long enough to explain how he killed a tankful of fish?

"Well, everyone forgets things," I say.

"I shouldn't have forgotten," Thomas says again. "When the aquarium was plugged in, it made a nice sound. Hmmmm-hmmmm-hmmmm. Like that. You can hear it in the aquarium store. It's so nice. When I unplugged the plug, the hum stopped. I knew the sound was gone, but I didn't remember why. My brain just skipped right over it."

"Don't beat yourself up," I say, and when Thomas looks puzzled, I say, again, "Everyone forgets things."

"Will you tell Dominique for me, Gabe?"

"I will, Thomas. I'm sure Dominique forgets things, too. He'll understand."

When Thomas and I are done bailing out the tank, we dump the water in his kitchen sink. Next we pour the gravel in the bucket, wash it until it looks new, and spread it—and the little diver figurine— out on newspapers to dry. Then I say good-bye and hurry back to the store.

No one is there but Dominique. I stand quietly for a minute after I come inside. I stop and listen. There's the humming. You don't really notice it unless you listen for it. But once you notice it, it gets into your head. It's actually sort of soothing. I guess Thomas finds it so soothing, he takes it everywhere he can, humming tunelessly like an aquarium when he's feeling happy. If only Thomas could stay in that bubbly-humming place—a place, it occurs to me, that Maxie manages to stay in most of the time—then maybe he wouldn't have to click and blink. Poor Thomas. Lucky Maxie.

Dominique has to know I'm here—a bell automatically rings when the door opens—but he hasn't said a word. So I do.

"Hi, Dominique," I call out. "Guess I'll finish up these e-mails and go home." I figure I'll talk to him about Thomas tomorrow.

"You finished up with Thomas?" Dominique asks.

"Yeah. It was no big deal." Then, since, as Dad always says, there's no time like the present, I tell him what Thomas told me.

This time, Dominique hears the story out. At the end, though, he doesn't react as I expect him to. He doesn't say, "Poor Thomas," or "Well, I guess I was a little hard on him," or "Maybe he should have a second chance." Instead Dominique frowns and exhales a big breath. And he says, almost under his breath, "You can't help some people."

I cry out, "Yes, you can!" and explain how easy it will be to help Thomas by helping him set up another fresh bubbly-humming aquarium. "And Dominique," I say, "I'll do most of the work. You can just supervise. Or I can do it alone with Thomas, if you don't have the time."

As I wait for his answer, I notice an opened letter on the counter: a cream-colored envelope with an official-looking seal as part of the return address. A terrible worry begins to form in my head.

Dominique sees me looking. "Yes, that's from the organization that awards the scholarship I've been waiting for," he says. His voice is so low I can barely hear him. "Only no scholarship for me this year."

"No!" I exclaim.

"Yup," he says. "It looks like I'll be here at Tanks for You in the fall. Again."

I don't know what to say. This seems to be happening to me a lot today.

Before I can say anything, Dominique speaks. "So, Gabe, I guess I'll have plenty of time to set up another aquarium for Thomas. If there's one thing I'll have, it's time."

Dominique flashes his teeth. But there's no joy or laughter on his face. This isn't a smile. It's a frown that came out the wrong way.

Chapter Fifteen

Take Your Marks

This morning, I'm not thinking about aquariums, or computers, or movies. No, today, it's all about swimming, and for good reason: My times for breaststroke have been, in a word, fantastic.

Not that I'm going to the Olympics any time soon. Not that I'm the next Michael Phelps or Mark Spitz or anything. (Especially since they didn't even swim breaststroke.) But I'm doing fifty meters in less than forty-five seconds, and that's better than anyone else on my team in my age group. And so far this season, it's been better than anyone else on the teams we've competed against.

Today, the first Saturday of August, we're having our final swim meet of the summer. We're hosting the team that holds the best record in our division—the team that also happens to have the guy who has clocked the fastest fifty-meter breaststroke in the eleven- and twelve-year-old age group. I'm with my teammates in the grassy area near the deep end of the pool, waiting to be called for my events.

"I've never been the best at anything," I said to Dominique yesterday, "and I'm probably not going to start being the best at something now. Especially not something athletic."

"Oh, man, what a tired old attitude!" Dominique said, and laughed. I shrugged and smiled. I smiled because Dominique was smiling again, and his voice was singing again, and his teeth were flashing again. He had felt so disappointed and angry when he didn't get the scholarship. It had been especially hard to take, I think, because he knows, inside, that he'll be an outstanding student who will go on to be an outstanding doctor.

But it doesn't seem to be in Dominique's nature to stay stuck in a funk. He told me he talked to his parents and to some of his professors at the community college and to his friends.

"I got my confidence back, Gabe, and that sort of squeezes out the anger. Also, why should I let people who don't even know me take away my confidence? That's *mine*, man. I shouldn't have let them have it for even a nano-second." Dominique had already apologized to Thomas for being so angry, and he promised that next week—when I'm all done with swim practices—he'll help me set up Thomas's aquarium again.

"Don't be so hard on yourself," he continued. "Or are you just practicing a little reverse psychology—talking yourself down so your hopes don't get too high, when deep inside you really believe you're a winner?"

Me? A winner?

"Your breaststroke is up in three events, Gabe." Don, our coach, taps me on the shoulder. "Evan, Brian, you, too." We're perched on those lounge chairs with vinyl webbing that leaves stripes on the backs of your legs.

"Let's go," Evan says. We make our way slowly to the check-in table, where we tell the mom who's in charge that we're the swimmers from the Rockwood Fins for the fifty-meter boys' eleven- and twelve-year-old breaststroke.

I'm looking around for the competition. Three boys from the other team—the Matapeake Marlins—check in for the same event, but I don't catch their names. One of them must be Timothy Fields, breaststroker extraordinaire, but I don't know which one. It would be good to know who he is, so I could keep an eye on him during the race and pace myself against him. But I can't just say to the three of them, "Timothy Fields, identify yourself!" I could ask the check-in lady, but now she's busy with another group of kids, and anyway the loudspeaker is calling us to the starting blocks. This is it.

"Swimmers, take your marks," the starter directs when everyone is in place. A pause. Then: *Honk!* The six of us dive in.

I know our teammates are cheering, but I don't hear a thing. After my dive, I glide as far as I can, holding my body in a tight streamline. Then I take a good hard pull underwater before surfacing to begin my stroke. Pull, breathe, kick, glide. Pull, breathe, kick, glide. Pull, breathe, kick, glide. I get into my rhythm, my groove, and then I hit the end of the first lap—pull, breathe, kick, touch—and push off for the second twenty-five meters.

After I come out of a long underwater glide, I steal a glance to my right. No one there. I look to my left, where I see the water currents from someone else's stroke and glimpse that swimmer's head bobbing in and out of the water. Pull-breathe-kick-pull-breath-kick—but that's his rhythm. Don't let it throw mine off. Just because he cuts his glide short, doesn't mean I should. Get into it, really dive into it, pull, breathe, kick, glide. Pull, breathe, kick, glide. With each pull and breath, I practically lunge forward into my glide. I'm back in the zone again, that isolated, underwater feeling where it's just me, the resistance of the water, and the wall beckoning from the end of the pool. I'm swimming away from a shark, a stingray, a barracuda. My legs pump the funny-looking frog kick, powering my glides. Go-

go-go-glide, go-go-go-glide, go-go-go-touch! I'm at the wall, which I slap with a two-handed touch. Made it!

"Nice swimming, buddy!" a timer in my lane says.

"Way to go, Gabe!" I hear Dad shouting. He says that whatever event I swim, however I do.

"Whee-yuh! Whee-yuh!" I hear Maxie's unmistakable cheer. And that's how I first know I won this race, two-tenths of a second ahead of Timothy Fields, the boy in the lane next to me.

Back on the deck, Evan and Brian, who came in third and fifth, slap me high-fives.

"Great going, Gabe," says Evan. He's happy for me and very happy with his third place finish. Anything but last, and he's satisfied.

We take our places back on the lounge chairs and sit quietly for a few minutes as our breathing slows down to a normal rate. The next race is beginning. I look for Don, who hasn't been by yet to congratulate us. He's over on the deck, but he's not watching the thirteen- and fourteen-year-old breaststroke race. Instead, he's deep in conversation with the referee, a man in sunglasses with a whistle around his neck. Don is shaking his head as the referee is talking, and the referee spreads his hands out as if he's saying, *There's nothing I can do. That's it.*

What's going on?

Don strides over to the grass where we are. "Great effort, guys," he says. But he's not looking particularly cheerful.

"Great effort, but what?" Evan says.

"Well. What happened is . . . there's been a ruling. Gabe, you were disqualified. The stroke-and-turn judge said you took two arm pulls with your head beneath the surface after the turn. That's an illegal stroke. You know, the rule is one underwater pull, then your head has to break the surface. The referee has disqualified you."

I don't get it for a few seconds. Then I hear Evan say, "Coach, what does that mean? That they came in first?"

Don nods. His face is pulled into a grimace. "Yeah. Gabe's win doesn't count."

"So I'm second?" I say.

"Not even that, I'm afraid. Your swim doesn't count at all."

"My time?" I ask. The timer said I clocked in at forty-three seconds flat, my best ever—and our team's record for the event.

"Your time doesn't count, Gabe," Don says. "I'm really sorry."

Doesn't count! I did not stay underwater too long.

Doesn't count! What kind of stupid rule is that? I do my best, I try my hardest, and it's not enough.

What do I have to do to win? Why is everything so *difficult* for me? I've wasted my entire summer on this dumb swim team!

My teammates are sympathetic and outraged for me.

"Stupid rule!"

"That referee must be seeing things."

"Tough break, Gabe."

I relive my strokes after the turn. I pushed off from the wall and had a good, strong glide. When did I look to the right and to the left? After the glide? After my second arm pull? I had a long underwater glide, a pull, and then surfaced and got back into my rhythm. My *legal* rhythm.

Or did I not break the surface in time? Did I stay underwater one pull too long? Underwater, where I feel safe, shielded from other people—whether I'm underwater in the pool, in my computer room, or just in my mind. Underwater I feel weightless, smooth, and easy—not *difficult*, not complicated, not edgy.

Did I stay under too long?

I don't have much time to think about it; it's time to get ready for my next event, the boys' relay. Our line-up is Zach Traynor, backstroke; Peter Stefano, butterfly; yours truly, breaststroke; Daniel Lee, freestyle. Sometimes we win this one, and sometimes we lose.

Coach Don comes over to give us a pep talk before we

check in. Zach, Peter, and I find each other and stand together. Daniel, whom I'm sure I saw on a lounge earlier, seems to have wandered off.

Before he reaches us, the coach stops to tap Evan on the shoulder. He says something to him that I can't hear, and the two of them approach our relay-team-minus-one.

"Okay, guys, we have a change in line-up," Don says. "Daniel is in the bathroom throwing up. So Evan here will join in the relay team today."

So far, this doesn't make a lot of sense to me. Daniel swims the freestyle leg of the relay. The coach is replacing Daniel with Evan, but Evan is terrible at freestyle.

"So listen up," Don continues. "I'm putting Evan in as the breaststroke man. Gabe, you'll be the clean-up man, swimming freestyle in Daniel's place."

"But—" I say.

"What's wrong with Daniel?" Zach says.

"Dunno," Don says. "He could be sick, or he could have gulped down too much water when he swam his fifty-meter freestyle event."

"But—" I say.

"I'm still butterfly? Zach's still backstroke?" That's Peter.

"Yeah. You guys are the same."

"But," I say, "breast is my stroke. I'm better than Evan at breaststroke. Why should I have to do my second-best stroke?"

The final call for our relay event blasts over the loud-speaker.

"They're coming!" Don bellows across the pool to the announcer. To us, he says, "Get going, guys!"

"But, *Coach*," I begin again.

"Go, Gabe," Don says. "Just *go*, will you?"

I go. At the starting horn, Zach leads us off with his powerful backstroke. He reminds me of a cartoon speedboat out there, his arms rotating like the blades of a motor, his head stretched way back so that it's almost upside down. At the wall, he neatly executes his turn, lengthens his lead on his push-off, and brings it home with hardly any let-up in his motorized pumping.

Zach touches the wall, two body lengths ahead of the Marlins' swimmer, and Evan dives in. His breaststroke looks okay, but his competition is the Marlins' Timothy Fields, who, after all, just beat us both in the fifty meters. At first, Evan's out in front, but that's only because Zach put him there. Once Fields hits the water, Evan doesn't have a chance. By the turn, Fields is ahead. He stretches out his lead on the way back, and by the time the two swimmers approach the end of their laps, Fields is five full body-lengths ahead of Evan.

When Evan finally touches the wall, Peter dives in the lane and starts to attack the water furiously with his butterfly stroke. Kerplunk, kerplunk, kerplunk—head up for air—kerplunk, kerplunk, kerplunk—head up for air. At the turn, he hesitates and loses a little time, as he always does. Butterfly is a very tiring stroke.

"Move it, Peter!" I hear Zach and Evan shouting behind me. I'm perched on the starting block, waiting for Peter to come home. I see the Marlins' freestyle man take off beside me once his butterfly swimmer is in. And then Peter touches and I'm off.

If breaststroke feels like deep-sea diving to me—quiet, smooth, easy—freestyle feels like running, no, make that *plowing*. It feels like hard work, all sloppy and slappy and splashy. It's not my style.

Slap, slap, slap, slap, slap, breathe. Slap, slap, slap, slap, slap, breathe. I do have good lung capacity. Because I can hold my breath for so long, I can go more strokes than a lot of kids without breaking my momentum to breathe. Here comes the turn. Now I wish I'd practiced flip turns with Zach, but it's too late for that—here's the wall. Just dive like you're evading a predator in *DeepSea*, become a submersible missile, somersault, and *EXPLODE!* off the wall.

I'm not sure about the submersible missile part—maybe it's more like a Zygurt drone. Missile, drone, or human, I shoot out of my turn. I see the white water of the Marlins' swimmer's kick just ahead in the next lane.

Push yourself! There's a tiger shark on your tail! That's a blue marlin ahead of you—catch it! Yeah, yeah, the marlin's one of the fastest creatures in the sea—catch it anyway!

Slap, slap, slap, slap, slap, breathe. Slap, slap, slap, slap, slap, breathe. Slap, slap, slap, slap, slap, slap, slap—wall!

My heart is beating wildly.

"Nice swimming, bud," says the timer.

"Way to go, Gabe!" I hear Dad shouting.

My teammates are screaming wildly.

And then I hear what I'm listening for.

"Whee-yuh! Whee-yuh!" Maxie.

I caught the blue marlin.

Chapter Sixteen

That Crazy Screaming

We've won the meet against the Marlins, by a narrow margin—four points, the number of points we edged ahead thanks to our win in the relay. After the Marlins leave, our team has a celebration at the pool with pizza, a big cake, and sodas. I get congratulated a lot, and I congratulate other people, too. It all gets kind of noisy and crazy. I find a spot on the grass, a little apart from the others.

But after a few minutes I'm bored and getting hot. I make my way to the deep end of the pool, where kids are playing a game of water polo. Maxie is playing, sort of, although it's mainly a bigger kids' game. He's a strong swimmer for a little guy. He can tread water for a good, long time. That's important in water polo, because you have to stay upright by treading water while you pass the ball or try to make a goal. Since the other kids are bigger, and water polo is kind of a hard game, Maxie seems to be spending most of his time hanging onto the wall. Still, like always, he's an enthusiastic team player.

"Here, here!" He urges his teammates to pass him the ball. "Over there, over there!" he coaches. Every so often Maxie gets the ball, but for the most part the big kids ignore him.

I lower myself into the water, but out of the playing field. As I get in, I notice Jake on the deck across the pool from where I am. He could pass for a swimmer even though he hardly comes to the pool. Jake is bent over the deck as if he is drawing; every so often he goes over to the pool to dip his hand in and then goes back to his drawing. I squint to see him better—he has a small paintbrush in his hand. He's painting with water on the deck. He looks totally into what he's doing.

"Whee-yuh!" Maxie's team has made a goal. "Whee-yuh! Whee-yuh!"

Funny how I actually listened for it at the end of my races, listened for it as a welcome signal of victory. But right now it's just Maxie's extremely annoying *Unnatural Force* shriek. It is unnatural. And it makes me feel all sharp-edged inside.

To escape, I dive under. How great it would be to go diving in the ocean, in the coral reefs off the coast of Bermuda. Dad's contest ends next week, and he says he's close to the level of sales needed to win the trip. Wouldn't that be great?

I surface briefly for a gulp of air, then dive under again. Underwater, I watch the water polo game. The sea of legs treading water reminds me of the underwater forests of giant kelp I've learned about in my *DeepSea Canyon* game. The strands of kelp grow from the ocean floor and they sprout like crazy, as much as two feet per day. They can be one hundred feet tall.

Up again for a mouthful of air, and then under. I love this feeling. But then I remember my breaststroke disqualification.

Forget it. Ha! Forgetting about bad things—floating above them, diving below them, whatever—has never been a big talent of mine. But maybe I'm getting better at it—or at least better at just moving on. Like today, I sure moved on when I swam freestyle in the relay.

I surface and glance over at the deck where Jake is doing his water painting—only he's not there. Then I look at the water polo field, which is nearly empty. But what's really strange is how quiet things are. Why have all the kids suddenly stopped their laughing and cheering?

Then I see why, and I almost stop breathing: Maxie is lying on his side on the deck. Jake is bent over him. And a lifeguard is running—*sprinting*—in the direction of my brothers.

Chapter Seventeen

Clear to the Bottom

I'm deep underwater—again—so deep there's no sunshine, no waves, no swooping gulls. There's just me, navigating through a forest of giant kelp in my round little bathysphere. Spiny, scary-looking fish swim nearby, along with a stingray, an octopus, and a dense school of mackerels or amberjacks. Rockfish are scattered on the ocean floor. A line of some sort—an air-supply hose? a cable to tug on in case of emergency?—connects my ship to a little boat bobbing up on the surface of the sea. In the boat are a man, a woman, and two boys. Way down in the deep, in water that's clear to the bottom, I'm smiling in the safe enclosure of my round little submarine.

At least, I'm pretty sure that's me in the bathysphere. I can't imagine who else Jake would draw exploring the depths of the ocean. Surely that's me, as I've described myself diving in my undersea computer games a dozen times—or maybe hundreds of times, because he never seemed to catch what I was saying when I explained the games to him.

I'm at the end-of-summer student exhibition at Jake's art school, and what I've been examining is Jake's prize-winning picture that he's entitled—ha-ha—Tanks-Giving Dinner. The joke is, the whole scene—ocean, boat, bathysphere—is set in a large aquarium that is set on a table in a dining room, where four people are sitting looking at the tank. You only see the back of their heads, at first, and then you see their faces reflected in the aquarium.

"Why 'Tanks-Giving Dinner'?" Maxie asks. He's standing at my elbow, which is itself a minor miracle, given what happened to him at the swim team party two weeks ago. Maxie had been playing in the polo game, staying close to the pool wall. When the opposing team just missed getting a goal by throwing the ball over near the chrome ladder that leads from the pool wall to the deck, Maxie saw his big chance. He figured he'd duck underwater and hit the ball from below. Only after he ducked underwater, Maxie's leg got caught in the ladder.

He couldn't free himself to get up to the surface. Maxie held his breath as long as he could, and then his breath gave out, and there he was, trapped underwater by the chrome ladder.

No one noticed. The polo players barely knew Maxie

was playing. And I was off in my underwater world. The life-guards also missed Maxie's disappearance in the crowded pool, and Mom and Dad were talking to their friends on the grass.

Jake was the only one who noticed Maxie's little body trapped underwater when he stepped over to the edge of the pool to dip his paintbrush in the water. And he didn't hesitate. Jake dove in, swam over to the wall where Maxie was trapped, untangled him from the ladder, brought him to the surface, and well, the rest is history. Next thing I saw, Maxie was on the deck, Jake was leaning over him, and a lifeguard rushed over to get the water out of Maxie's lungs. The lifeguard had him sputtering up pool water in no time.

Jake. In his own way, definitely some sort of hero.

"Why 'Tanks-Giving Dinner'?" Maxie asks again.

"Well," I begin. I can't take my eyes off the picture. It looks watery, but not drippy. I lean in to read the small print under the title on the card that's taped to the wall next to the picture. "Jake Livingston. Gouache on paper."

I pronounce it "GOO-awk on paper."

"Gwash," Jake says, joining us. "Weird spelling. It means a special kind of watercolor with some sort of gum added to it. I like it for water scenes. Plain water colors are too—watery, I guess, for me."

"Gwash," I repeat.

"*Gwash*," Maxie says. "*Gwash*. Like, *Gwash*, what a great picture!"

Jake and I groan, and we explain the Tanks-Giving joke to him. Maxie cracks up. "Tanks—Thanks! I get it! Tanks for thelling me! I mean, thanks for telling me!" He finds himself hilarious and goes off, laughing.

"So, Jake, that's me, isn't it?" I ask. Not that it looks like me. But no one in the picture really looks like anyone I know in real life.

Jake looks at the picture. "Well . . . sometimes."

"Sometimes?"

"Sometimes you're the one underwater. Sometimes you're in the boat. Sometimes you're around the table. But it's not always you underwater. It can be anyone—me, Maxie. Mom or Dad."

"Oh," I say. And here I thought I had this picture all figured out. "What's the line there? An air hose? A rope?"

"Yeah. Both. Either. Whatever makes you feel safe." Jake has a dreamy look in his eyes. "Whatever keeps you connected to the surface."

Uh-huh. Okay. Whatever you say, Jake. You're the artist.

Jake leaves me standing there staring at his picture while he visits some of his classmates' exhibits. I look at the smiling boy in the bathysphere. I can imagine why he's smiling—because he's off on this own, away from his family, friends, enemies, exploring the unknown. And because he's got that cord, that hose, that whatever attaching him not to the bottom of the ocean, but to the surface. If the explorations become too dangerous or he gets tired of being alone, he just needs to tug on the cord.

Dad, Maxie, and I are going home. Mom will stay with Jake until the show closes, in an hour or so. I'm planning a new strategy for *DeepSea Canyon*. Maxie has something else on his mind.

We're driving home in Dad's car. "Please, Gabe, can we work on a movie? I'll help you. I'll move guys, hit the lights, hold the camera, whatever you say."

I consider his offer. There's a new video camera at home. It's what Dad won from his office's Bermuda program instead of a trip to Bermuda. He finished the contest just one sale short of the big prize.

"Bermuda will have to wait, Gabe," he told me at breakfast the morning after he found out he didn't win.

"Oh, man!" I wailed.

Then we crunched our cinnamon toast in our usual silence, and Dad went to work.

I was disappointed, but I made myself think of Dominique waiting another whole year before he gets another chance at a scholarship. Bermuda and snorkeling could wait, too. Meanwhile, I—that is, we—have a new, state-of-the-art video camera.

"I'll be your helper," Maxie is still wheedling in the car. "And you'll be the next Steven Spielberg."

Yeah, right. Where'd he get that, anyway? Dad pulls into the driveway. The three of us get out of the car.

"Okay, Gabe?"

"Well," I say as we go up the concrete steps to the front door, "how about if I'll just be the next Gabe Livingston?"

"Yay!" Maxie says.

I could have said I'll be the next Donald Duck, and Maxie wouldn't have noticed. All he knows is we'll be making a movie, and he'll help. That's good enough for him.

I won't lie and say it's good enough for me, too. I still have high ambitions. But if Steven Spielberg looks over his shoulder, he won't see the next Steven Spielberg coming toward him. Or the next Jacques Cousteau. He'll see the next somebody. He'll see me.

About the Author

DEBBIE LEVY is the author of children's books and poetry. She has written about subjects ranging from sunken treasure to U.S. presidents, from the Vietnam War to the Berlin Wall. She used to be a lawyer and a newspaper editor before writing for children, and she's glad she made the switch. In her free time, and even when she's busy, Debbie likes to kayak and fish on the beautiful Wye River. She lives in Maryland, where she and her husband raised two sons, a dog, and a cat. Visit her website at www.debbielevybooks.com.